Sorcha

Sorcha

UNITE

Volume Two of The Sorcha Books

Susan Alford & Lesley Smith

Illustrated by Candy Alford

ISBN: 0692064540
ISBN 13: 9780692064542

Dedication

To our parents, Delton and Myrna, for your DNA, for having our backs more times than we can count and for always believing our "someday" would come.

Acknowledgments

• • •

"Be around the light bringers, the magic makers, the world shifters, the game shakers. They challenge you, break you open, uplift and expand you. They don't let you play small with your life. They remind you that a blip in the road is just that, a blip. These heartbeats are your people. These people are your tribe."

~Danielle Doby

To our children, Kaity, Cara, Emma, Noah & Ansley: You are the best things we ever did in our lives! You have shared this journey with us from the start and it would have been much less colorful without you.

To our soulmates, Del & Andy: Your love, patience, encouragement and support have never faltered. Thank you for not just believing, but knowing that we could do this.

To our friend, Brian Conn: You have been an endless source of critique and ideas during the final stages of writing this book—we dedicate all the unchecked tears and strikes of lightning to you.

To Axel Arzola and Lucas Hicks: A huge shout out for your creativity, vision and design skills!

To the Crew (Austin, Ben, Kenzie, Kaity, Jon, Cara, Aaron, Emma, Bostick, Ashley, Lucas, Danai and David): Here's to cold dark nights running through woods and tunnels, cheeseburgers, costume changes, laughter, and ridiculously good times!

To our readers: You have embraced the Sorcha and joined us on our journey. We will be forever grateful. The hard work that went into making this series a reality is worth it because of you.

To our Father God, His son Jesus Christ and the blessed Holy Spirit: You created us with gifts and blessed us with purpose. You have inspired, guided and ordered our steps along this incredible journey. To you, the Light, we give all glory, honor and praise.

Visit www.thesorchabooks.com and follow us @thesorchabooks on Facebook & Instagram

"The issue is now clear. It is between light and darkness and everyone must choose his side."

~ G.K. Chesterton

"So Jesus said to them, "The Light is among you only a little while longer. Walk while you have the Light, so that darkness will not overtake you. He who walks in the darkness does not know where he is going. While you have the Light, believe *and* trust in the Light, have faith in it, hold on to it, rely on it, so that you may become sons of Light, filled with Light as followers of God."

-John 12: 35-36 AMP

Contents

Prologue

• • •

Light and dark.
Love and hate.
Life and death.
What are they all?
Just two points lying at either end of a narrow winding road?
I think they are so much more.
You see, I believe we all have a light and a darkness living inside
us.
Good and evil war in our hearts, minds and souls.
We struggle.
We are tempted.
We resist.
We overcome.
But, nothing is hidden.
Nothing is secret.
The light reveals all.
It's clear to me now because I know what moves in the darkness.
We aren't alone in this world or the other.

Hunted like demon prey, there is nowhere to run or to hide.
Our destiny is written but our fate is unclear.
Will we bear the light of goodness and hope?
Or will we be swallowed deep into the malevolent darkness of power and greed?
We all must choose a side.

CHAPTER 1

Bars

• • •

DUBLIN, IRELAND

HE OPENED HIS BLOODSHOT EYES and groaned. His mouth was dry— his head pounding. He rubbed his face feeling the roughness of his day's growth of beard. He didn't know how long he had been passed out on the king-size bed in the luxurious hotel suite. He didn't really care. Even though too much living and too little rest were taking its toll, Aiden needed to lose himself in the blur. He had only been in Ireland for a couple of weeks, the fourth stop on his spree of destruction across Europe. It had been two months since the battle in New York and no matter how much he tried to forget, the events of that day would be forever etched in his mind.

He grabbed his phone to look at the time— 8:00pm. He would have to hurry if he was going to make the fight. He rolled out of bed and headed for the shower. The hot water cleansed his body but not his mind. He was already revved-up for what was to come. His jeans, t-shirt, boots and supple black leather jacket complemented his dangerous mood. He left his room— the predator ready for his prey.

Outside the hotel, he climbed on his motorcycle and roared through the dark streets of Dublin heading toward the outskirts of town. When he arrived at the abandoned distillery, a rush of adrenaline coursed through his body. His senses were heightened— his anticipation growing. He entered the building through a heavy metal door. He descended the steps into another world.

"It's about bloody time! The crowd is restless," the beefy man in the woolen cap reproved.

Aiden's dark look silenced any further quarrel even though the man was twice his size. He walked down the dimly lit hall removing his jacket and shirt. He tossed them nonchalantly at the burly man trying to keep up with his long strides. He was focused, deadly calm— ready to begin. He flung open the double doors and was met by thunderous applause. He strode purposefully through the wild crowd towards the iron cage. Some people were taunting and cursing, while others whistled and bellowed his name in wicked glee. Aiden had made quite a name for himself in Dublin's underground fight circuit these last two weeks. He was now the one to beat; he was the sure bet. His lethal skill and cunning strength were an unbeatable combination, especially when there were no rules.

He removed his boots and stepped into the cage. It was a boxing ring inside an impregnable fortress of thick iron. The door was slammed shut and chained behind him. It was literally a death trap. In the cage, fighters could use a mixture of martial arts to take down their opponent. It was full-contact combat. Tonight, like every other night, it would be a fight to the death. And Aiden felt right at home.

Stadium bleachers, for spectators, circled the cage. Their cheers were deafening. Aiden turned slowly in a circle giving the crowd what they wanted— a better look at him. He was the main event! Their attention only sharpened his focus. Then, he sized up his opponent.

He had the look of an Irishman, reared by the very streets of Dublin. He was fair-skinned, about 6' 2" tall, bearded and brawny in an understated way. He was tough as nails. Aiden knew immediately that this man would be a worthy adversary. His steely green eyes were full of determination and something else Aiden couldn't quite put his finger on. When his opponent exchanged a meaningful glance with a fresh-faced young man with ginger hair, standing outside the cage, Aiden knew. The young one's eyes and face were so similar to the man he was getting ready to fight, Aiden decided the two must be brothers. He sensed something was definitely wrong. The younger brother was held firmly despite his struggle between two hefty men. That could only mean one thing— his rival was fighting for a cause, and that made him dangerous. Aiden smiled— this was gonna be fun.

The bell rang signaling the beginning of their deadly dance. The crowd vanished— their shouts silenced. For Aiden, there was only the Irishman and nothing else. He wasted no time in his frontal attack. He was quick but the Irishman was methodical taking his measure, deftly dodging his jabs.

Aiden pushed ahead striking with an incredible combination kick. The Irishman stood his ground. He returned Aiden's attack with an outside left kick and then a jab to the midsection. Aiden laughed— finally— a challenge. The two warriors fought, returning blow for blow.

Aiden took the Irishman by surprise and drove him up against the cage. When the Irishman spared a glance toward his little brother, Aiden went in for the kill. He muscled the Irishman down to the mat trapping him in a chokehold. The Irishman strained against Aiden's death grip to no avail. Aiden knew his rival's strength was spent— he had run out of options. A sweet sense of victory filled Aiden's dark soul. Death was so liberating. Death was his savior.

The Irishman turned his eyes toward his little brother outside of the cage. The boy was yelling. The men holding him drug him out of the room through a thick metal door. Aiden looked at the Irishman, his eyes full of pain. He had failed himself and Aiden figured even more the Irishman had failed his little brother. It meant nothing to him! Aiden squeezed applying a tremendous amount of pressure to his fallen opponent's throat. When the Irishman's eyes rolled back in his head, Aiden jumped up and raised both arms in victory. The crowd roared violently.

A hulking force slammed into him from behind, knocking him to the ground. The Irishman had risen. Aiden cursed himself for not finishing the job. He wrestled with the Irishman but was quickly overpowered. But not before he saw a telltale symbol behind the Irishman's ear. He sucked in his breath.

He gave no recourse when the Irishman picked him up and threw him bodily across the cage. Then the Irishman went to the thick iron bars and pulled them apart with his bare hands. The crowd roared in disbelief. Aiden watched the Irishman exit the cage and run to the heavy metal door his brother had been taken through. He ripped it off its hinges and threw it easily aside and disappeared. Things had just gotten very complicated.

CHAPTER 2

Enemies

• • •

LUCAS HIT THE BRAKES HARD. His vintage Mustang, a gift from his father, skidded to a halt at the end of Parker Street. The sun was beginning its ascent in the eastern sky—the faint glow of soft orange rays that should have brought warmth to a new day only solidified for Lucas the reality of what had been lost and all that must be gained. Beyond the stop sign in front of him was the risk, danger and even death. If he crossed the invisible and supernatural boundary of the Centenary College campus, he understood he would be fair game for the demons who hunted him and his friends.

Inside the perimeter of the school was the sanctuary of the Sorcha and the stronghold of the incredible legion of guardian angels who protected them. This was the only place he was safe. Since his escape along with the other Light-bearers from New York City, he now felt a burden of responsibility so great it threatened to overwhelm him. For now he would have to wait, frustrated, within the shelter of Centenary, until the rest of the Sorcha were discovered. Tomorrow, the fall semester would officially begin. Just like any other ordinary college student, he would go to his first class, buy his books, maybe even, study. Lucas smiled to himself at the irony of it all. Thousands of students, living on campus and attending classes, all totally oblivious to the supernatural battle raging around them.

The cool of the morning couldn't mask the horrible stench wafting through the atmosphere just beyond the perimeter. Lucas could smell the hideously beautiful creatures—like death—only a hundred yards away. They waited for the smallest mistake, the tiniest opening and then they would attack with a ferocity unlike anything Lucas had ever known. He sensed an intense energy outside the boundary of Centenary—rabid and unyielding. Cain was coming for them, still masquerading as Flynn Talbot, Cleveland's famous and wealthy entrepreneur. But they knew his true identity, the commander of the demon army of Scáths, and the right hand of Abaddon himself. The Light-bearers, with the help of the Dìonadain guard, had thwarted Cain in New York City. Lucas knew Cain must be furious.

Though the loss of Aunt Scarlett had been painful for his family, Lucas knew they had been lucky to not lose more that day. The next time, Lucas feared, Cain wouldn't be so easy to defeat. Cain would not give up. He didn't like to lose. He would do everything, both naturally and supernaturally possible, to kill Lucas and the others before they could unite the powers Elohim had gifted them to destroy all that was evil and dark in this world. Unfortunately, Lucas knew that time was on Cain's side. Each day without the discovery of the rest of the Sorcha was yet another day without finding the key to Simon's book and the location of the book itself—another day of danger and possible death for all the Light-bearers—another day the uniting of the Sorcha would not happen.

Lucas got out of his car and walked to the invisible boundary, its low-key hum indistinguishable to all but him. As the Perceiver, he was gifted with the power of discernment—his sensitization to the supernatural world enabled him to see what others could not—both good and evil lay within his awareness at all times. Lucas lived in two worlds, and the pain caused by the collision of these worlds two weeks ago was still raw and deep. His best friend, Aiden Talbot, had betrayed him. Aiden had fooled Lucas and his sister Lily into believing he was a good person, one who loved them both. But it had all been a lie. Aiden was evil to his core. He was the son of Cain and sister to Lysha, the demon assassin also known as Keket. Lucas would never forget the cold blue flames burning in his friend's eyes or the otherworldly way he had moved when he attacked them in the tunnels. He could almost feel Aiden now outside the perimeter watching him, daring him to break free from the sanctuary.

"Soon, my friend," Lucas whispered, "We will settle what is between us."

The disappointment of Aiden's betrayal and the senseless murder of his Aunt Scarlett had hardened Lucas. He looked forward to the fight to come. Yes, the Sorcha would unite. Yes, they would find the key to Simon's book and the book itself, unlocking the secret to defeating the demon armies. And along the way, he would meet Aiden and make him pay for his lies, his rejection, and the incredible pain he had caused his sister. Lucas wanted to defeat evil, yes, but more than that, he was resolved in his mind to destroy Aiden Talbot.

"Your feelings about Aiden will destroy you, Lucas," Nolan said gravely. "Your anger and unforgiveness will only poison your mind and your ability to do what Elohim requires."

Lucas turned around and met his guardian angel's stern gaze. "Aiden will pay for what he has done, Nolan."

"Vindication is Elohim's, not yours. There is still much for you to learn if you are to be strong enough for what is to come. The others need you to focus on what is at hand."

"I have never been more zeroed in, Nolan. I know what I'm fighting for."

Nolan studied him as if searching for the truth of his heart. Lucas couldn't decide if he should stare back at Nolan's deep blue eyes or try to square off with the hundreds of pairs of eyes embedded in Nolan's massive shimmering wings. Wherever Lucas would turn his head, the eyes would follow him. It was quite disconcerting.

"I think it is time you see what you are fighting for," Nolan said, seeming to make up his mind about something.

When Nolan gathered him close within his wings, Lucas knew it was time for one of Nolan's surprise field trips. Since he had lost his father to the Scáths' attack in the woods all those years ago, Nolan had been taking Lucas on these journeys, teaching and guiding him in the exploration of his gift.

Lucas struggled within the cocoon of Nolan's wings. "Hey, Nolan, I can't see. Your wings, man, move your wings.

Nolan chuckled, "I know the way. No need for you to see in the natural. Use your gift and look beyond, Lucas."

"Where are we going this time?"

Nolan whispered softly, "Home."

CHAPTER 3

Citadel

• • •

WITH THAT WORD, LUCAS WAS blindly rocketing up and up through the air, safely hidden within Nolan's wings. Lucas focused his senses, looking beyond the anger in his heart for Aiden, beyond the rush of wind indicating the speed of their ascent, beyond the soft heaviness of the feathered wings tickling his face, and beyond his anticipation to see where they were going. Instead, he breathed deeply and turned within. The moment he stilled his mind, he was flooded with emotion and thoughts so deep, rich and pure, he could barely breathe. Joy. Peace. Contentment. He had never felt such a strong wash of emotion before—it permeated his very being.

"Look now, Lucas," Nolan commanded softly.

Their flight trajectory had leveled off. They were soaring still high above the ground but were now slowly circling a wondrous sight below. It was a place beyond human imagination and creativity—simply breathtaking. A majestic fortress rose into the air from a large island. Surrounding the island was an expanse of ocean as far and as wide as Lucas could see.

The crystal sea shimmered with schools of luminescent fish and sea creatures. Waves crashed upon the jagged white cliffs that ringed the island.

"It's shaped like a star," Lucas mused in wonder.

"This is my home, Lucas," Nolan announced reverently. "The Citadel of the Dìonadain."

Five strong, circular towers, or bastions, twice the height of the vast walls, which must have been at least twenty feet thick, surrounded a larger stone cavalier rising from the center of the star-shaped stronghold. All were fashioned of golden stone. Tall thin slits were arrayed across the walls in perfect symmetry. At the pinnacle of the center structure was a light shining so brightly Lucas could only describe it as a white-hot star. It pierced the thick clouds of the purest white and gold above and pulsed with great energy. A mammoth golden angel, holding a flaming sword in his hand guarded the entrance to the cavalier. The angel had four different faces—a man, a lion, an ox and an eagle. He had two sets of wings—one pair covered his body while the other was out-stretched behind him.

"I've never seen anything like him," Lucas breathed in awe. "He's terrifying!"

"He is the mighty cherubim who guards the path to the gates of Shamayim, the Kingdom of Heaven, the seat of Elohim and his heavenly creations. The portal of light beyond those doors is the path to the gates of heaven. The gates are closed to us now. We will not venture there until Elohim commands it," Nolan instructed.

"So, the Citadel defends the entrance to Elohim's kingdom and the cherubim guards the path to its gates?" Lucas asked.

"It is as you say," Nolan responded.

"Wow," Lucas breathed reverently. "Holy ground. Thank you, Nolan, for bringing me here."

"You are seeing what few have ever, Lucas. Your gift allows this, do you understand?"

"I am beginning to," Lucas answered. "Our Creator is above all, literally."

Nolan smiled, "Indeed."

"There in the bastion at the main gate is the Great Hall where the Dìonadain gather every morning and night to pray and to hear from Elohim. The Dìonadain Council meets there as well to strategize and direct our armies. The remaining four bastions of the Citadel serve as headquarters for the separate divisions of the Dìonadain.

"I remember," Lucas responded. "The Watchers monitor the movements of the Scáths, the Messengers search for the Sorcha and relay all communication to the council."

"And the others?"

"The Warriors fight the Scáth armies, and finally there are the Guardians. Twelve super-soldiers, special forces if you will, who guard and defend us, the Sorcha."

"We work together toward our common goal—the annihilation of darkness in this world."

"Look at that," Lucas shouted, pointing in the distance.

A great winged bird, an eagle, with its strong muscular legs, powerful talons and incredible wingspan swooped down from above them and alighted on top of one of the Citadel's bastions. Like a sentry, it scanned the horizon marking their approach.

"What's going on down there?" Lucas asked. The sound of metal clanking and the roar of voices below was unmistakable.

"You're gonna love this my boy," Nolan chuckled. "Better than the movies, I promise."

When they landed softly on the ground, Nolan's wings unfurled slowly from around him. Lucas wobbled trying to maintain his balance, so great were the sights and sounds around him. Nolan steadied him. Lucas could only stare in amazement. The field surrounding him was alive with the sights and sounds of battle. The Dìonadain were training and it was an awesome sight to behold. It was almost more than one pair of eyes could take in at a time. These massively built combatants were the Dìonadain Warriors. Lucas studied them as they moved adeptly through their battle dances.

Artfully they ducked, dodged, and parried each blow delivered by their opponents. The clang of golden metal echoed in the busy yard. Sparks flew off the weapons at impact. Others around the yard practiced their skill with the bow, firing arrows into targets with lightning speed and precision, while others, riding astride war horses, clashed with sword and shield. Their movements were being watched closely by a large warrior garbed in dark bronze armor. His voice boomed across the pitched field. Lucas knew this must be Andreas, the commander of the Warrior division of the Dìonadain. Nolan had told him stories of this gifted fighter.

Andreas raised a hand acknowledging them, then bellowed, "Nathan! Dara! Show the braw lad how it's done!"

The combatants in their burnished armor drew glowing broadswords. Lucas' heart sped up anticipating the events about to unfold. He was about to witness a clash beyond legend and myth. These weren't just any skilled and accomplished soldiers but warriors of the Light—there was no comparison. This was going to be epic!

Nathan and Dara circled one another taking each other's measure. Nathan attacked quickly, but Dara side stepped his offensive. Dara countered but Nathan met her advance thrust for thrust. Both, equally matched, were magnificent and agile. When Dara's blade glanced off Nathan's bronzed armor, she leapt into the air avoiding his responding charge. Her massive wings created a whirl of dust around them. Lucas eyes stung but he was afraid to drag them away from the warriors for even a second.

Nathan roared charging into the swirls of dust. Lucas could hear Dara's responding laugh. They were enjoying this! Nathan whirled around to block Dara's attack and returned a thrust of his own. She parried and began to pivot, but she was too late. Nathan was already there at her back, the tip of his gleaming broadsword pushed against Dara's exposed throat. She dropped her sword. Nathan smiled in triumph. But the fight wasn't over. Lucas could see it in Dara's eyes. Nathan was enjoying his victory and had let his guard down. When Dara winked at Lucas, she confirmed his thoughts. Dara grabbed Nathan by the throat and slammed him to the dirt. Her action was met by a thunderous roar of approval from the warriors in the yard, beating their swords against their shields.

"Well-done my warriors! You are the first line of defense for our Light-bearers. Take no prisoners, aye?" Andreas commanded.

"I could hang out here forever," Lucas smiled. "It's like XBOX on hyper-drive."

"Come, I want you to meet my brothers and sisters—the Dìonadain Guardians," Nolan said.

Lucas followed Nolan as he strode around the cavalier at the center of Citadel to the other side of the yard. Nolan's heavy wings drug the ground behind him. The eyes always watching Lucas from Nolan's wings were closed now. Lucas was just about to ask Nolan why when he caught a glimpse of five warriors training along the eastern wall of the Citadel. They were dressed in the golden armor of a Dìonadain Guardian. These elite warriors would be the protectors of the remaining five Sorcha, once they were located. Each wielded an unusual weapon while also wearing the Dìonadain golden broadsword at their hip. Their fighting styles differed because of the weapons and nature of their combat.

"They are magnificent," Lucas breathed.

"War requires warriors, Lucas. Elohim has trained our hands to war and our fingers to fight."

Lucas knew to describe their movements as graceful didn't do them justice. Rhythmic yet fluid— intricate yet simple— beautiful yet lethal—the Dìonadain guardians were incredible to watch. Their disciplined movements and powerful presence set them apart from the other angels training in the courtyard. Where the Dìonadain warriors were the ruggedly fierce hammer; the Dìonadain guardians were the sleek fiery sword.

"Tell me about them, please," Lucas asked, never taking his eyes from the spectacle.

"Makaio prefers to meet the enemy wielding his great talayalu."

"A war club," Lucas speculated. "I've read about them. It was the weapon of choice for a Samoan warrior, right?"

"Yes," Nolan answered. "His opponent, Ehud, is the master of the spear and bashing shield."

"Like Hector in those awful Greek tragedies I had to read in school? I have to admit, Ehud is way cooler, live and in person," Lucas mused. "The blade on that spear must be at least a foot and a half."

"You should see him with a sling shot!"

"Seriously? Like David and Goliath?" Lucas asked, a definite man crush showing in his expression.

"Seriously," Nolan answered, his smile stretching across his chiseled face.

"Wow, again," Lucas exclaimed. "And he's left-handed to boot! What about hers? That's the most wicked looking weapon I have ever seen."

"The Ngombe Ngulu is Imani's favored weapon. She would appreciate your admiration; she too thinks it is the most wickedly lethal weapon ever forged. However, my brother, Shen would disagree. He would rather meet a Scáth on the field of battle with his katana than use his broadsword on any occasion."

"And the angel throwing the daggers?"

"Ah yes, well…"

A loud horn sounded full and deep interrupting any further explanation from Nolan. Immediately, the guardians stilled their movements and turned toward the entrance to the Citadel. Through the raised heavy iron portcullis thundered a lone rider on a winged horse whose coat was so shiny it looked like golden metal. The rider's light-colored leather jerkin with golden buckles, long fitted pants, supple dark leather boots, close-cropped close hair and golden short sword strapped to his side marked him as a Dìonadain messenger. Lucas figured by the expression on the rider's face, he was the bearer of some pretty important news.

The messenger dismounted quickly and strode purposefully toward the center of the training field. He bowed his head in respect to Nolan and then announced curtly, "I have news, sir."

"Tell us, Samuel," Nolan commanded softly.

Lucas felt his heart beating out of his chest. Maybe, this was it. Maybe, the other Light-bearers had been found. He could sense the great anticipation in the guardians standing around him as well. They were poised—alert.

"Would you like the good news or the bad news first, sir?" Samuel said wryly.

When Nolan remained silent, the messenger continued, "Right—very well then, another Light-bearer has been found, in Ireland. However, the Mescáth, Aiden Talbot, is already in play."

"Good work, Samuel. Inform Jude and Ira at Centenary. They are to meet us in Ireland with Lily and Daniel," Nolan commanded.

Samuel mounted his winged horse and thundered back through the gate.

"Ehud, you know your path," Nolan said. Ehud left immediately leaving a blazing golden trail across the sky.

"Makaio, you and Shen are with me," Nolan finished his commands.

The guardians, Makaio and Shen, glowed hot, their strength and readiness for battle pulsing through their bodies, their weapons and their massive wings.

"What about me?" Lucas asked. He was afraid Nolan would leave him for safe-keeping here in the Citadel. But Lucas wanted nothing more than to enter the fray and confront Aiden.

"We need your gift, Lucas, not your anger," Nolan said.

"Shouldn't I be angry? Besides, my feelings toward Aiden have made me even more determined and passionate for the success of our mission. What's wrong with me hating the darkness that's destroying the ones I love?"

"You are fueled by the wrong emotion because you are driven by the wrong objective, Lucas. That is the crux of the problem. You see, our mission is not to eliminate the darkness. We exist to liberate and illuminate the light. When the twelve unite the Light within them, the darkness will have no place to hide. I need to know if you can put your feelings aside and focus on the mission. Can you do this?" Nolan asked urgently.

"Yes!" Lucas replied, quickly burying his anger deep in his gut where it would be contained at a slow burn.

Lucas understood Nolan didn't need an angry young man full of revenge right now. He needed a Light-bearer imbued with Elohim's power and strength ready to use his gift in the ongoing battle against the darkness that was surely rushing to Ireland right now. He met Nolan's hard inquisitive stare with one of his own. Something in his eyes must have convinced Nolan. Lucas let out the breath he had been holding when his guardian enveloped him in his wings and left the heavenly realm and the Citadel far behind.

• • •

Time stood still here.

The cold mountains had hidden them for centuries.

Deep within their snowy sanctuary, the Natsar, her people, thrived.

For the first time, she would venture beyond her home.

Her grandfather had received a message from the Citadel.

There was hope for a uniting.

Perhaps their wait was over?

Patience had been her constant companion.

Now, she would need wisdom to be her guide.

Her grandfather had kissed both her cheeks in farewell.

The road set before her was perilous.

She might never return.

But that was of no consequence.

Her purpose, if the Light-bearers were found worthy, was to guide them home.

She tossed her pack across her shoulders and didn't look back.

Black trees, charcoal caricatures against the dove-white drifts, were the silent observers of her passing.

Just like them, she would watch, from a distance, until it was time.

CHAPTER 4

Thunder

• • •

Ioan Taryn thundered down the basement hallway after his younger brother and the armed men who held him captive. He gave no thought to the massive amounts of adrenaline coursing through his veins, his straining muscles that hummed with electricity or even his shocking ability to pull the thick iron bars of the cage apart as if they were rubber bands. He didn't consider he might be outnumbered, that the men who held his brother were surely armed and dangerous, or even that he might be facing his own death. He only knew he had to reach Jamie before it was too late. He had failed him before— miserably. But not this time. He would rescue his brother, and they would run hard and fast, far from their miserable life.

The Taryn brothers had seen more than their fair share of suffering in their young lives. Born four years apart, Ioan, quiet and melancholy, had always played the role of caretaker to his charming and precocious little brother, Jamie. He had had no choice really. Their da, Hugh Taryn, was a cold-hearted beast of a man who drank far too much, loved not even a little and enjoyed nothing better than using his wife Bridget and her boys as his punching bags. Hugh worked as a derrick hand on an oil rig spending months away at a stretch from his family stacking drill pipe high above the deep waters of the Irish Sea.

While his father was working, Ioan, Jamie, and his ma enjoyed a simpler more peaceful life. Ioan went to school with friends, prayed at church and played ball with Jamie in the backyard of their small cottage. The laughter and happiness of the three of them together held the pain and violence at bay for a time—until his da would return. Ioan came to dread the bleak and defeated look that would color his mother's bright eyes when she knew her husband would soon be returning.

Always, the night his da would come home from the sea, his ma would bake Ioan's favorite shortbread cookies and bring them into the boys' room before tucking them in for the night. Although he loved the sweets, he knew they signaled the darkness that his father brought with him. During his short life, Ioan had witnessed too much hurt—too much violence. It had made him tough on the outside but inside he was bewildered and desperately sad. Why did his da treat them like he did? It wasn't right! It wasn't fair! Ioan wrestled with his powerlessness to change their situation, and a slow burning anger grew inside him at the injustice of it all. His mother's words, difficult to swallow, were always the same.

"Ioan, your da is a fierce man but he loves us in his own way. The drink makes him angry about life, you see. He wanted so much more than what we could ever have. But we must live as we must, doing the best that we can. And love, Ioan—always we must choose love. Remember, the good book says to turn the other cheek and that is what we will do," Bridget vowed.

Leaving the cookies on the table by their bed, Bridget would lock her boys in their room for the long night. It was her way when they were but small lads. To mask the sounds of his da's shouting and his ma's crying, Ioan would tell Jamie fantastic stories of adventuring pirates who sailed the Irish Sea. He held Jamie's hand, singing crazy songs from the radio, whatever he could think of at the time, until his brother fell asleep. But as Ioan grew taller, bigger, and stronger than his father, he took his mother's place. He never fought back, taking his father's blows, remembering his mother's words and knowing that with each hit, his mother and brother were protected. But that had all changed one night six years ago.

Ioan, just shy of his 19th birthday, came home from his work at the docks later than usual, to find his mother broken and bloodied in the middle of the kitchen floor. His father's handprints were rough and red on Bridget's throat. Her eyes were open, staring lifelessly back at him. Jamie was slumped beside her, his left eye purple and swollen shut, blood seeping from a gash across his forehead. His small wiry body shook violently as he wept and held his mother's limp hand. Neither mother nor son had been able to defend themselves against Hugh's violent drunken rage.

Ioan's body tensed, his hands fisted tightly, his teeth clenched willing, the sight before him to disappear. She was gone. He would never again hear her sweet voice, feel her gentle touch or see her bright smile again. His eyes found his father across the room. Hugh was just standing there in the corner sniveling like a lost pup. His father's false bravado was gone. The horror of what he had done was now real and raw before him if his anguished cry was any indication.

"Oh, what have I done?" he bawled. "I didn't mean to hurt my Bridget. I didn't know—please, son, believe me…"

Ioan crossed the room in one movement, yanking his simpering father up off the floor by his collar.

"You murdered ma, you bloody animal!" Ioan raged.

Gone was the quiet submissive older son. Here now was a brawny young man filled with incomprehensible rage and grief. He shoved his father roughly into the dark corner. With each hard pummel of his fist, Ioan relived every slap, kick, and punch his father had exacted on him, his mother and his little brother. He didn't see his father. He only saw his father's heart—cruel, cold, and destructive. He wanted that heart to stop beating—he wanted the evil that was his father gone forever. An urgent hand pulled back on his shoulder giving him pause.

"Ioan, please—stop," Jamie said with agitation. "You're killing him."

Ioan let Hugh's limp body fall to the floor. His father's breathing was labored, his face a bloody pulp. Ioan fell back into a chair. What had he done? He was no different than his father to use such violence to assuage his anger. He stared dully at his mother lying cold on the floor. Was this even real? How had it come to this? If he had only come home sooner? He would have been there to stop him. He had failed the most important person in his life.

Numb with grief, he slowly unclenched his fists, studying the blood and broken skin across his knuckles. He hadn't kept his word to her. Instead of showing love he had given in to his rage, almost killing his father. He was no better than that beast. No matter how awful Hugh had been to them all, Ioan had dishonored his ma by not turning the other cheek. His wretched mourning sobs filled the room.

The next few days were a blur. The police, seeing the horrible reality in front of them when they arrived at the Taryn home, had arrested his father. Unfortunately, Hugh Taryn had built quite the reputation for himself as a vile and brutally vicious malcontent. No one doubted that Ioan's injury to his father was in self-defense. Hugh Taryn was sentenced to life in a prison for his crime. His sons buried their beloved mother, leaving a single white rose on her grave. The brothers left their village on the coast and moved to Dublin searching for peace and perhaps a new beginning.

But instead of gaining perspective and finding their way, Ioan couldn't deny that he and Jamie had lost themselves on the streets of Dublin. Hungry and without shelter, he had been desperate to provide for Jamie. He had sought work wherever he could but it was never enough. They had been three days with nothing in their bellies, when, dejected and hopeless, he and Jamie had found their way into a run-down pub one night on Sheriff Street. Too much to drink and a bar brawl later, Ioan found himself with a pocket full of cash and the assurance of more. He had earned a name for himself that night "Son of Thunder" because of his heavy punches and lightning quick speed. He hated that his fists were Jamie's ticket to a normal life. But, he would not fail his brother again. He would give him the respectable life he deserved.

Five years later, Ioan was making enough money running drugs and cage-fighting for the Gallagher crime family that he could send Jamie to a proper school and rent a flat in a trendy area of Dublin. He was busy and often gone, but he knew it was necessary if he was going to give Jamie a chance at a better life. His little brother was resourceful, charismatic, and too confident for his own good. After Jamie was caught skipping school and selling exam answers to the highest bidder, Ioan thought it best to enroll him in a school far from Dublin. He knew his brother needed to be away from Ioan's job, lifestyle and the less than reputable people that populated his life. They were obviously influencing Jamie in a less than positive way.

But Jamie had had other plans—after a blistering row, his brother had left Ioan's flat like a thief in the night and disappeared into thin air. Ioan hadn't seen him in two months. He had scoured the city for his brother, asking everyone he knew, and that was a lot of people in his line of work, but to no avail. He was afraid that Jamie was lost to him forever.

Until last night, when a knock at his door brought Ioan the worst news possible. Jamie was alive, yes, but he was in deep trouble. His little brother had put his knack for making things to good use it seems, only it was the wrong things—bombs— for the worst people—the Madigan crime family—the rival faction in Dublin and sworn enemy of his boss Seamus "the Monk" Gallagher. The Madigans had employed Jamie, attracting him with fancy words of praise and the promise of fame and power. Jamie was a sucker for adoration and attention. He slid down the slippery slope into a life of crime without a thought for caution. But Jamie was impatient. In his bid to be noticed, he had made a fatal decision. He betrayed the Madigans and sold his high-tech bombs to no other than the Gallagher family. Now Monk Gallagher was nothing if not an opportunist, so when he realized that he was doing business with Ioan Taryn's little brother, he decided he would use the Taryn brothers to his advantage and strike the Madigan family where it would hurt the worst, their pockets. The Monk already had Jamie and his bombs, but he wanted much more. He wanted to destroy the Madigan family—strip them clean of all their monetary assets and crippling their ability to run a business in Dublin for any longer. So, he struck a deal with Ioan.

The word on the street was that the Madigans had a weakness for gambling and had a dangerous amount of cash riding on the victory of their recently acquired champion fighter in tonight's cage bout. If Ioan defeated the Madigans' champion in tonight's bout—the Gallaghers would win big striking a blow where it would hurt their rivals most—their cash flow. If Ioan won, Jamie would be freed and forgiven. If he lost, well then Jamie would surely die. Ioan had pleaded for mercy—for the life of his stupid selfish brother. But, his pleas fell on deaf ears.

Ioan had no choice. He had come full circle. His brother's life hung in the balance. His mother's words echoed faintly in his head as he barreled down the hallway in pursuit "…always choose love, Ioan…" He was choosing love—his fierce love for his brother—he wouldn't let his ma down this time.

He roared through the exterior double doors into the dimly lit parking lot.

CHAPTER 5

Hope

● ● ●

AIDEN PUSHED THROUGH THE RAUCOUS crowd, climbing the stadium seats swiftly. He touched the heavy metal door lightly as he passed through, wondering at the giant whose Samson-like strength had torn it from its hinges. The sign of the Sorcha behind the strong man's ear was undeniable. He had seen the same mark behind Lily Quinn's ear only months before. He exhaled painfully. She plagued his thoughts—waking and sleeping. Just one fleeting thought of her was tantamount to an excruciating kick in his gut. Before that fateful day in New York, he hadn't known how impossible it would be for them to ever share their lives—their love. He hadn't realized that Lily, as well as her brother, Lucas, his best friend, were both his mortal and supernatural enemies—the Sorcha.

As a Mescáth, he was sworn to destroy the twelve Light-bearers for the power they bore within them. Only the twelve Sorcha when united together could discover and retrieve the ancient book written by Simon the Zealot that held the secret to the destruction of evil and all of his kind. His love for Lily didn't matter. His brotherhood with Lucas was meaningless. At least, that's what he had been telling himself every waking hour for the last two months.

Although he struggled wanting desperately to just see Lily one more time, he was sure it wasn't the same her. He frowned remembering her shock and then the revulsion that shone hotly on her face at the battle in New York City when she was faced with the truth of who and what he was. He had lost Lily Quinn—the love of his life—forever. In his present reality, there was no room for love. Love was weakness. Love was light. He was the darkness. He was evil. Only pleasure, power, and greed had meaning in his stygian world. Now, he embraced the shadows within him. He was created to be a hunter—a killer—and that was his destiny.

Aiden knew his father, the mighty demon Cain, commander of Abaddon's demon armies, must know already of the awakening of another Sorcha. Using the artful persona of Flynn Talbot, internet mogul, his father had access to information around the globe. His Scáth spies were everywhere gathering and transmitting information to Cain's high command post. Nothing escaped his knowledge or his influence. Even now, Aiden counted on the fact that his sister Lysha, his father's favorite child and conveniently lethal assassin, was enroute. But, his father and sister would both be surprised and disappointed. This Light-bearer was his find, his acquisition. Even though it had happened by chance with no manipulation or strategy of his own making, one of the twelve had fallen into his hands and he would claim the credit and the kill.

When he heard the roar of the Irishman, he slowed his movement and slipped soundlessly through the door out into the dark night. He crouched behind a nearby dumpster and viewed the landscape, calculating his next move. The distillery was behind him. The old granary building loomed large across from him in the clear moonlit night. The overgrown ground between the two buildings was uneven and riddled with trash and broken pieces of glass from whiskey bottles made long ago. Closer to the granary building, two dark SUVs were parked with engines running—their headlights illuminated the space. The two burly men from the cage arena held the young man, the Irishman's brother, one on each side. He wasn't struggling, in fact, he had a slight smile on his face as if he knew his big brother was going to wreak havoc at any moment and he couldn't wait to watch. In front of the little brother's captors, was a row of able-bodied men with guns drawn and aimed at the strongman.

"This should be fun," Aiden chuckled under his breath.

The Irishman's back was to him. But Aiden could tell he was laser-focused on the task before him, considering the barely leashed fury that marked the Irishman's stance and straining muscle. Here, before him, stood a Light-bearer in full expression of his gift: supernatural strength. He was impressive. If Aiden was honest, he would admit he was a little envious of this man's light. But the Light within the Irishman would be no match for his own darkness, fueled by his need to prove himself to his father.

Aiden would have to think quickly in order to subdue him and take him down. He frowned when a low rumble of thunder filled the space and a crack of white-hot lightning pierced the clear sky. His sister was coming. He needed to make his move. But the Irishman had already entered the fray, using the surprise of the lightning to his advantage. He was making quick work of the armed men who stood between him and his little brother. The louder the Irishman roared, the faster he worked and the stronger he became, it seemed. Smashing faces, throwing bodies, breaking bones, and obliterating guns. It all happened within a few seconds.

Aiden grinned as he watched the beautiful destruction. He wouldn't have to do anything but wait for the Irishman to get to his brother and then they would both be his for the taking. The little brother's two captors looked scared now. One ran as a coward will do, while the other tried to pull the little brother in front of him as a shield, but he was not successful. The Irishman was too quick. He shoved one of the SUVs toward the captor with such a mighty force, he was knocked to the ground and run over before he could even respond. The Irishman's brother had rolled out of the way, seeming to understand his brother's tactic at just the right second.

When the Irishman helped his little brother up from the ground, Aiden took his cue. Soundlessly, he ran from his vantage point behind the dumpster and came up behind the brothers. Lightning shot across the sky again. Aiden couldn't wait any longer. His flaming blue eyes sparked and he extended his hands shooting darts at the little brother, dropping him to the ground. He pounced on the Irishman from behind, taking him down swiftly. His opponent struggled but was imprisoned tightly in Aiden's flaming blue embrace.

Thunder shook the ground. His sister, Lysha, and her minions surrounded him and his captive. But she was Keket now, the Mescáth—fierce, brutal, and glorious in her beautiful lethality. Her long braid hung heavy down her back. She had brought a full contingent of Scáth warriors with her—all seasoned and hungry for Sorcha blood. But, they were too late. This was his kill—his first.

"Little brother, aren't you just full of surprises?" Lysha teased. "I've missed you. Father will be so pleased."

Aiden nodded his head slightly and increased the pressure of his flaming cords around the Irishman's neck. He barely noticed when the little brother crawled away from the fray. What a coward! He was worthless.

"What a beautiful Light-bearer he is," Lysha mused bending down and running her red-nailed hand over the Irishman's short cropped hair. His eyes flashed with fury in response to her touch. "A pity I didn't find you before my brother did."

"He's mine, Lysha. Back off!" Aiden snapped.

"Touchy, aren't we?" Lysha stood and studied the sky. "The Dìonadain are coming. The air has shifted." Jerking her gaze back to him, she spat, "Well, what are you waiting for? If you are going to take his life, do it!"

Aiden focused on the Irishman's eyes, he wanted to see the hope extinguished from them as he squeezed the life from his body. He had been conditioned physically and psychologically for this moment. His father had exacted a heavy price from him during his training each time Aiden hesitated to take a life. He knew he was a disappointment to his father when he struggled to wield the cold fury that pulsed within him. It was his destiny to kill. It was his birthright as a Mescáth. Although the jagged physical scars he received from his father's merciless floggings when he failed healed instantly, the deeper, more complex psychological ones plagued his mind like a seeping wound.

Aiden felt a piercing pain sear through his body. He released his hold on the Irishman and fell back. He looked down to find a dagger fashioned of whiskey glass deeply embedded in his shoulder. He was dumbfounded until he saw the little brother throwing the same daggers at the Scáth warriors around him. Aiden was wrong, the little brother wasn't a coward after all but another Light-bearer. He had crafted lethal weapons out of the broken pieces of whiskey glass that lay around them. The young one's gift must have emerged in response to his desire to save his brother's life. He had underestimated both of the Irishmen.

His sister screamed with frustration. He knew what she was thinking. Another Light-bearer meant the Dìonadain when they arrived would be in full force. They were quickly losing the advantage.

Lysha motioned to her demon warriors to create a perimeter around them. They followed her command, circling them, flaming darts at the ready, chanting in their hideous language. Lysha's eyes flamed and hot blue orbs of light pulsed in her palms. "You are mine, Light-bearer!" she vowed as she stalked toward the little brother.

Aiden had no time to watch as the Irishman who at first was shocked by his little brother's attack now turned his attention and full-strength back to him. Aiden leapt to his feet prepared to fight. The Irishman flexed his chest and roared at Aiden. Aiden pulled the glass dagger from his shoulder and tossed it away.

"Let's see what you can really do, Irishman," Aiden taunted. The same blue orbs that had flamed in his sister's palms now leapt in his.

When the Irishman charged him, Aiden lunged throwing multiple darts from his hands toward the Irishman. They found their mark riddling the Light-bearer's flesh with burning embers. But the Irishman didn't slow his advance. He slammed his body into Aiden knocking him back several yards with the force of the hit. Aiden kept his balance, hot anger surging through him. He was done with this fight. It was time for the Light-bearer to meet his creator. Aiden catapulted into the air over the strongman and landed behind him. He slammed his palms together and his eyes roared with intense blue flames. It would be a lethal blow to the Irishman; Aiden's flaming darts would now be thick arrows of annihilation so destructive and powerful that no human, not even a Light-bearer could survive them. When he turned to exact his final attacking blow, Aiden stopped dead in his tracks.

She was there—standing right across from him—only thirty yards away outside the Scáth perimeter. Lily Quinn, the beautiful girl who held his heart and who haunted his days and his nights, was here—watching him—willing him, just like that day in New York, to choose the light and not the darkness within him. By her side was her guardian, Jude, the Dìonadain warrior who existed only to protect her. His armor glowed hot in the darkness of the night. His flaming sword was drawn and at the ready.

The ground shook violently as twenty golden Dìonadain warriors catapulted from the sky and surrounded them. Their spectacular wings waved in the air creating a rushing wind that leveled the Scáths to the ground—rendered motionless in an instant. Aiden watched nonplussed as Lysha turned from her attack on the Irishman's little brother and with an almost imperceptible turn of her hand she shot a large flaming blue orb around the Scáth perimeter. As the orb passed over each Scáth, the ground beneath roiled and swallowed the demons whole, sucking them deep into the earth where they would be protected from any further Dìonadain attack.

Aiden looked back at Lily. Behind her, to her right was Daniel, the Believer, his arms outstretched praying for the strength of the Dìonadain warriors in the fray. His guardian, Ira, was busy deflecting Keket's offensive advance. To her left, was Lucas, his best friend, struggling but restrained by his guardian Nolan. He could feel Lucas' anger—hot and slicing like a knife to his gut. Yet, it all faded to nothing when he looked at her. Even as the Dìonadain closed in, he stood there unable to tear his eyes from hers—wishing he was not who he was, hoping she could find a way to forgive him—loving her even though he knew she hated him. But her eyes were filled with disdain for him. Her revulsion wounded him more deeply than any of his father's beatings ever had. But then there was something else in her hot gaze—just for a moment—but something he didn't count on. It was regret. And that was enough to plant a seed of hope in his black heart—one that he would go to the ends of the earth to nurture and realize.

"Aiden," Lysha shouted. "To me!"

In that frozen second, Aiden knew if he was ever going to see Lily Quinn again, if there was ever any chance of winning her back, he would have to move. Together, brother and sister were stronger—their powers of darkness greater and more —they needed each other if they were going to escape the Dìonadain guard surrounding them now. His sister, astute strategist that she was, recognized that they were significantly outnumbered and needed to run and live to fight another day.

Understanding her command, he nodded his head. Aiden leapt into the air propelling himself toward his sister as Lysha did the same. When they collided a giant coil of blue flames curled around them, scorching the ground below. A bolt of white hot lightning shot jaggedly across the sky and brother and sister disappeared within it.

CHAPTER 6
Ribbons

•••

LILY STARED AT THE EMPTY space where Aiden had just been. She couldn't deny that the pain of his betrayal had shaken her. But, the fruitful seeds of love that had been sown in her heart for Aiden had been ripped from her heart and trampled on in one quick moment in the bowels of the Dragoni building two months ago. She wouldn't be a fool twice. She had opened herself up to Aiden—been vulnerable with him. She had allowed herself to trust him and to experience for the first-time feelings of attraction and connection with him. That was a big step for Lily considering for most of her life she had avoided feeling altogether. Because of her past, Lily had decided feelings were just too painful—too fickle—too difficult to control. When emotions had threatened to overtake her, Lily had withdrawn, pushing them down deep into her soul.

But then she had met Jude—her friend and her guardian. He had protected her and given her the safety and encouragement she had needed to open herself up to feelings and to Elohim. Her dedication to Elohim and His plan for her life had changed her. She was learning to be exactly who she was meant to be—a confident young woman not afraid to show or experience her emotions—a brave young woman focused on training and using her gift in battle—a wise young woman who understood the power of a choice and the consequence of that choice. Her choice was Light. Her choice was family. Her choice was and always would be Elohim.

Something lying on the ground where Aiden had just been standing caught her eye. She bent to pick it up. It was the red ribbon she had been wearing in her hair the day Aiden had taken her to the mill. He must have kept it all this time. She shook her head. After their escape from Centenary, she had taken off the earrings Aiden had given her at Christmas and put them away forever. It didn't matter if Aiden still had feelings for her. It didn't matter if she wished things could be different. Because they weren't. He wasn't good for her and he never would be. He was darkness. She was light. He was a Mescáth. She was a Sorcha. They had been doomed from the beginning. She felt Jude beside her. Her guardian took her hand and squeezed it lightly. Lily knew Jude understood her hurt but also her resolve to move on. She had made peace with the truth of the Talbots, but Lucas obviously had not.

"Are you serious, right now?!" Lucas shouted angrily running over to join them. "We had them and we just let them get away."

"Your distemper is understandable, Lucas," Jude said, "but ill-placed. It is not for us to argue with Elohim's plan or His timing."

"Jude is right, Luc," Lily implored. "Look at who we have gained, the Warrior and the Crafter. We are closer now than ever to uniting the twelve."

"I know you're right but that doesn't mean I have to like it," Lucas muttered.

"No, it doesn't. But, you can't let your anger and hurt prevent you from seeing the big picture. We have a battle to fight. There are people depending on us to do what is right and to succeed, and that is bigger than either one of us or our feelings about Aiden. You got it?"

"Since when did you become the big sister, all wise and in charge?" Lucas said with a grin.

"Since always," Lily responded lightly and hugged her brother.

Sirens echoed in the distance and were getting closer. "Looks like the cavalry is on the way," Jude said wryly.

"We need to get back to Centenary," Nolan ordered. "We have much to share with our new friends. I'm sure Ioan and Jamie have many questions."

Lily rubbed the yellow ribbon between her fingers and then quickly tucked it in the front pocket of her jeans. Aiden had kept it—all this time. But why? What did that mean? Before she could reason any further, Jude wrapped her in his wings.

"Ready, Lily?"

She looked up into the eyes of her protector and felt immediate peace. She didn't need the anxiety that thinking about Aiden caused. She resolved to put it behind her and focus only on the future.

"Let's go," she replied, a big smile on her face, and then laid her head on Jude's shoulder.

Before Lily could count to three, she was in the yard of her Aunt Audrey's house on the grounds of Centenary College. Lights were glowing in the window of the old and newly restored Victorian house. Mia was waiting on the porch for them. Lily knew her mother would have been pacing and praying the whole time since the messenger had arrived with Nolan's orders for her and Daniel to get to Ireland.

Mia hurried down the steps to meet them. After exchanging quick hugs, she announced, "It's supper time. And Audrey's got a big spread. She knew y'all would probably be famished."

"And she was right," Lucas responded. "But, I think Daniel needs food more than I do right now."

One look at Daniel and Lily couldn't help but agree. The energy Daniel expended on their behalf in his prayers to Elohim for their power and safety was incredible. She knew that Daniel had been spending more time in prayer and even fasting meals these last weeks. Although Daniel looked a bit tired, his ever-serious eyes were full of joy. Lily knew he was pleased with their success tonight. Her respect for Daniel was great. He was the glue that kept them all together and focused.

Daniel met her eyes before he followed Lucas inside. An understanding passed between them. When a big grin spread across Daniel's face, Lily felt like she had been given a rare gift.

Lily laughed. The danger of just moments ago was passed. She was home. Safe and in the arms of her family and friends. "Thank you for protecting me, Jude."

"Always, Lily." Jude replied. "Nolan needs some time with the new Light-bearers to explain everything. He will bring them to the house soon. Will you tell your mother?"

"Yes, of course," Lily replied. "We're close, aren't we? To the uniting?"

"Yes, and that means there is more danger now than ever," Jude responded gravely. "If you have the dream again tonight, call out to me, Lily. I'm never far from you. Rest easy and enjoy this time with your family."

And with that Jude and the other guardians vanished. Lily followed the sounds of laughter and the smell of fried chicken into the house. Everyone was gathered in the big kitchen. Audrey had prepared a feast. Along with her famous fried chicken was macaroni and cheese, baked beans, cole slaw, hot biscuits, sweet tea and apple pie for dessert.

"Fix your plate, Lily," Audrey encouraged. "But save some room for pie—I made your favorite. And then come tell us the real story about these red-headed brothers. Lucas has got to be exaggerating."

Lily loaded up her plate and joined the others at the kitchen table. "Hmm, let's see. They are brothers. They are Irish. One is broody in a tragic Heathcliff sort of way while the other is always smiling. They are hot. Need I say more?"

Everyone laughed. And then, she continued, "No joke, these guys are remarkable. Ioan, the older one has strength you cannot even imagine and the younger one, Jamie, he's like dad. He can craft a weapon out of anything. Super cool—they got serious skills."

"Brothers! And one is red-headed to boot!" Mia exclaimed. "Well, I can't wait to meet them."

"Zoe is gonna be crushing hard. You better watch out, Beni," Rafe joked.

Beni blushed a little but ignored the ribbing from Rafe. Zoe threw her napkin at Rafe and giggled.

"People, have we forgotten why we are all here in the first place?" Wei asked.

"Not with you around to remind us all the time," Rafe retorted. "Lighten up, Wei. We need to be able to laugh every now and then. It reminds us of what we are fighting for."

"You're right, I guess New York is still on my mind," Wei said pensively.

"It's on all our minds, Wei," Lily agreed. "Right, Daniel?"

"Yes, we have much loss to grieve, but we need to celebrate all we have gained as well. We are smarter now. We won't be fooled so easily," Daniel offered.

"And we have a better understanding of what we are up against, too," Lily added.

"We've worked hard and we are better than ever at using our gifts," Beni said. "And, best of all, our family is growing. We found the Warrior and the Crafter, both in the same night. Only three more Light-bearers and our group will be complete," Zoe said.

"I believe when we unite our gifts, the real battle begins," Daniel stated quietly.

"Daniel is right," Lily agreed. "We haven't even begun our fight yet. New York was nothing compared to what will come. Don't you think so, Lucas?"

"Yes, and it will be soon, I feel it."

"I'm ready to fight!" Wei said passionately.

"You and me both, sister," Rafe chimed in. "Those Scáths aren't gonna know what hit them when we unite!"

"So, Lily, why don't you tell me and Zoe more about those hot Irish brothers," Wei teased, grabbing her third biscuit.

Lily was so happy to be home. She treasured these times around the table, laughing, the darkness lurking around them seemingly far away when they were all together like this. When Ioan and Jamie arrived with Nolan, Lily watched as everyone greeted the brothers, welcoming them into this wonderful family of theirs—the Sorcha. Daniel and Ioan hit it off from the start. Lily figured it was natural since they were older than the rest, but watching the two young men from such vastly different backgrounds and experiences converse with one another, she knew it was more than just age that drew them together. Instinctively, Lily believed Ioan and Daniel were drawn to the strength they recognized in each other. Daniel possessed an enormous amount of inner strength and control of the mind and spirit, while Ioan possessed the same measure except his was seated in his physical form. Both were marked by a seriousness of nature that was beyond their years—protectors of family and defenders of the weak. She was grateful for the gifts of these two.

She turned her attention to the other Taryn brother— Jamie. Although, he shared the same coloring as his brother, the similarities between them stopped there. Jamie was gregarious, high-spirited and loved to tell a good story, if Zoe's laughter and attention to him were any indication. Where Ioan was serious, Jamie was outgoing. Where Ioan was muscular and large in stature, Jamie thin and short. Where Ioan was soft-spoken, Jamie was loud and the life of the party.

"You saw him, didn't you?" Beni asked softly. He had quietly moved to sit beside Lily without her even noticing.

She shouldn't have been surprised. Beni was empathic. He always knew when one of them was struggling with something and didn't want to let on.

"I'm ok, really I am. It was so very strange to see him. He was so different than the Aiden I thought I knew. He almost fooled me again, though. The way he looked at me. It was almost as if he still cared—like he wanted my help. But, that can't be. We all know now what he is and what he is capable of."

"Yeah, but that doesn't mean it isn't hard to accept it. I know you cared for him."

"I did but I don't anymore. I'm not that girl—the one who pines away after the bad boy thinking that if she loves him enough, gives him enough, is perfect enough, he will change and be good. I've got more respect for myself and who I was created to be than to fall into that emotional trap," Lily said with passion. "At least, I pray that I do."

Beni put his arm around her shoulders and gave her a simple hug, "You do. And I believe in you."

"Alright, kiddos, let's get everyone settled. Classes start bright and early in the morning. Y'all need your rest," Audrey announced.

"Everyone but us," Zoe suggested mischievously. "Beni and I aren't going to school in the morning."

"Think again, sweetheart," Audrey answered waving a brochure in her hand. "Just because you and Beni can't leave the grounds of Centenary doesn't mean you aren't going to school. I registered you both in an online program this morning!"

"For real, Aunt Audrey?" Zoe asked looking at Beni with a grimace.

"Absolutely for real," Audrey responded with a smile. "And, you better be downstairs and ready to begin by eight o'clock. Sleep sweet, my darlin'."

The party came to a quick end after that. Audrey took the brothers to their new room. They would share the basement space with Rafe, Beni and Lucas. Audrey's room was on the main floor. The rest of the girls were all upstairs. Zoe was sharing her room with Wei while Mia and Lily had their own rooms. It was a big house with plenty of room for everyone. When the house was quiet and everyone was tucked in for the night, Lily snuggled deep beneath the covers. Mia had left a nightlight on in her room knowing that if her daughter woke from a dream, especially one laced with darkness, it would be reassuring to her.

Lily prayed for clarity before she drifted off to sleep. Nolan had warned her that her prophetic dreams would come more often and be more visually and emotionally charged the closer the Sorcha moved toward the uniting. Soon, as she grew stronger in her gift, her dreams would become visions—pictures of the future flashing before her waking eyes with no sleep required. She closed her eyes—her mind empty—her soul prepared for what she knew would come.

CHAPTER 7

Raindrops

• • •

"No!" LILY SAT UP ABRUPTLY, her chest heaving with desperate sobs.

She reached for the glass of water she always kept beside her bed and gulped it down. The cool liquid steadied her nerves. Seven nights in a row, she had dreamed of him. Each night her dreams of Aiden more vivid than the one before. Alone here in her room with no one to hide from, Lily wondered if they were rooted in prophecy or just the yearnings of her naive heart.

She wanted Aiden to be a good man, but there was no doubt in her mind or spirit that nothing could be farther from reality at this point. He was a Talbot and just like his father and sister—Aiden was evil. The Talbots were the enemy. Even if Lily wanted to forget that truth she could never forget that. It was because of Aiden's family that Lily's father and aunt were dead—murdered at the hands of demons.

The conflict she felt was only intensified when she compared the two very different versions of Aiden in her dream. When the dream began, Aiden was a small boy. He was full of smiles and had a head full of dark curly hair. He was with a beautiful woman who also had the same dark curls except hers was very long, tied back with a yellow ribbon. The two were at the beach playing in the sand by the water. The woman must have been Aiden's mother. Every so often as they played, little Aiden would reach up and curl a strand of his mother's hair around his chubby finger and giggle. It was a loving and carefree picture of a mother and her son.

But then the dream changed. The sky darkened and lightning flashed. Aiden started to cry. His mother gathered him close and tried to escape the storm but she couldn't move. Her feet were buried deep in the sand and she couldn't pull them out. The ocean waves grew bigger and bigger until they finally crashed over the woman, the strength of the waves pulling her under. Lily could sense the woman's desperation—her desire to hang on to her son. But as the waves pulled her deeper, two hands pulled Aiden out of her arms and the opposite way. Straining for her son and her son reaching for her, the woman disappeared beneath the churning ocean. The hands that pulled little Aiden from the depths of the sea belonged to none other than Aiden himself. Except he was grown and just like he was in New York City, cruel, blue-flamed eyes and a cold heart.

What did her dream mean? If anything? Why couldn't she just accept who Aiden was, a murderous monster?

She needed some air—a change of perspective. It was too early to wake Mia or the others. She knew Jude was close but wanted to mull the dream over in her mind by herself for a bit. Quiet as a mouse, she made her way down the steps and out onto the back porch. The sky was still dark. It was raining—a slow, gentle, end of summer soaking rain. She sat in the porch swing and let the back and forth movement bring a sense of calm predictability to her spirit. She reviewed the dream again in her mind trying to make sense of it and the possible message it held for the future of the Sorcha.

A sense of dread filled her when she noticed something in the distance. Audrey's house and yard were circled by a white fence that served as the delineating line between safety and danger. The property backed up to a large expanse of woods that were not protected by the Dìonadain shield. Two small matching blue flames flickered just beyond the fence of the property. It was Aiden. She knew it—felt it.

Against her better judgement, Lily left the safety of the porch and walked toward the blue flames in the distance. The rain was falling gently now but enough to soak her t-shirt and shorts through before she made it across the yard to the back fence. There he was standing in the rain, expressionless yet watchful as if he was ready to bolt at the slightest risk of discovery. His hands were shoved in the front pockets of his jeans—Aiden Talbot, soaking wet and still as devastatingly handsome as ever.

"Why are you here Aiden?" she asked.

"I had to see you. We need to talk."

"We have nothing to say to one another—not anymore."

"Lily, please give me a chance to explain. I'm sorry about your aunt, truly I am. But I had no choice. You have to see that? He is my father. He is so powerful."

"We all have a choice, Aiden. You chose the darkness."

"Lily, honey, please. We can just forget New York ever happened—at least in time. Come away with me. We can leave tonight—right now. No parents—no duty—no light and dark—just us."

"I'm not going anywhere with you, Aiden. Whatever I felt for you is dead now."

"You don't mean that, Lily. The way you looked at me in Ireland. I know you still care for me."

"Don't mistake love for pity, Aiden. For a moment after New York—a long one actually—I hated you. You betrayed me. You lied to Lucas and to me. You hurt me more than you will ever know. But, then, I realized you could only hurt me if I gave you that power. So, I forgave you."

"Ok, then let's start over. I promise you can trust me. We just need to leave this place and start a new life."

"We can't. We are destined for this, Aiden. I am a Lightbearer. There is no life for us beyond this. And I will never allow the darkness that swims in your soul to come into mine. You made your choice and I have made mine."

Aiden advanced but was halted by the protective perimeter. He grimaced with the pain of singed skin. In an instant, Jude appeared in all his golden glory—wings spread wide, sword drawn in defense of Lily.

Aiden swore, his eyes flaming blue. He moved to a defensive position.

"I should have known you wouldn't be far away," Aiden spat at Jude. Then he turned to Lily, "I know you love me. You know it too. It doesn't have to be like this."

"Yes, it does," Lily said softly. "I can't save you Aiden."

"Leave, Aiden. You are not welcome here," Jude commanded.

"Do you want me to go?" Aiden asked softly.

"Yes," she whispered and in a moment, he had disappeared into the dark woods.

• • •

Troubled, she watched them from the shadows of a magnolia tree.

The boy's irrational feelings for the girl were a problem.

One that could destroy the uniting of the Light.

She wanted to stop him. Needed to stop him.

The boy, Aiden, was evil—a monster of the worst kind.

One who took whenever and wherever it was convenient.

One with no awareness of anything but his own desire.

Lily Quinn mattered nothing to him.

She was a prize to be won, or taken if need be.

But the Quinn girl would be difficult to win over.

The Light-bearer was full of hope and purpose.

She wanted to make sure the boy failed.

But that wasn't her duty.

She was the watchman on the tower not the warrior at her gates.

CHAPTER 8

Crazies

• • •

AIDEN'S ANGER THREATENED TO OVERWHELM him. He slammed the front door to his father's palatial antebellum estate. The house was quiet. His father would not return until sunrise. He hadn't seen Lysha since the debacle in Ireland. The great clock in the foyer chimed the hour. He caught his reflection in the floor-to-ceiling mirror at the end of hall. Soaked to the skin, furious over his lack of control over his life and tormented by a girl who wore a red ribbon in her hair, he howled in agony. He couldn't stand to look at himself.

It wasn't supposed to be like this. Lily Quinn was meant for him. He knew that beyond any doubt. In fact, it was the only truth in the web of lies he and his family spun on a 24/7 basis. At a dead run, he barreled down the hall toward the mirror. The force of his fist shattered his reflection into a thousand pieces. The truth of who Aiden Quinn really was and what he really wanted was gone in an instant—replaced by the empty nothingness of a merciless killer with a cold cruel heart. Warm sticky blood dripped on the mahogany floor. He closed his eyes, drew a shaky breath and remembered his shame.

It was in June. He had just given Lily the earrings—diamond stars for his star. He was happy when he boarded the Talbot jet to fly to the mountains to meet his father and sister for their annual vacation. He couldn't wait to tell his dad about Lily—about his feelings for her. He had had no idea what was waiting for him when he arrived at their home located in a remote area of the Crazy Mountain Range in Montana, known as the "Crazies". It was a turning point. His life had changed irrevocably, and there was no going back.

He couldn't close his eyes now without remembering every vivid horrible detail of his birth as a Mescáth. In the deepest darkness of the pit, in the bowels of the Crazy Mountains, his father, Flynn, had revealed himself for the first time as Cain, fallen angel and leader of demons. Aiden remembered his absolute shock and disbelief. He resisted the truth but it became undeniable when he saw what his father could do. When Cain told him what he was—a Mescáth, and what he was meant to be—an assassin, Aiden had resisted again.

Lysha had made sure he understood that he had no choice. She explained to him that his mother had been a Light-bearer. Cain had stolen her away and forced her to conceive a child— one that would possess both the power of light and dark. Once she had served her purpose, Cain had taken her life. Aiden could still hear his scream of agony when faced with the truth of what his father had done. A part of him died that day realizing that the family he had loved and looked up to had taken away the only pure and good thing he had ever had in his life—his mother.

Now, it was Aiden's turn. Before he could embrace the darkness within him and channel the power of the Light given to him by his mother, he must be cleansed. He fought as hard as he could to resist—to escape—to withstand the agony of the cleansing. But he had failed. He could still feel the heavy iron shackles around his wrists, ankles, neck and waist—the horrific heat of the fire—icy, flaming jolts of blue electricity coursing through his body. He could still smell the repugnant scent of brimstone coming from the vile demonic beings that circled him endlessly. He could still hear their bloodthirsty shrieks and bellows—a never-ending chant that filled his mind and soul with so much darkness that every shred of happiness or goodness that was in him was completely sucked out.

At times, Aiden would be released from his shackles. His Mescáth brother, Kayanja, would escort him out of the pit and into the house. There in a room made entirely of windows, where the view of the Crazies was magnificent and colors of the summer day were vibrantly hued, Aiden was commanded by his father to kill. Each time it was a different person—tied up, gagged, their eyes full of fear and pleading for mercy—a woman, an old man, a child. It didn't matter. Each time Aiden had refused, Lysha had done the deed herself while he was made to watch. Then, Kayanja, his Mescáth brother, would beat him mercilessly.

When Aiden had felt the whip slice across his back, he vowed to become stronger. And he did. He had steeled himself against the pain—willing himself to hold on until he could escape. He let the anger and resentment he felt toward his father and sister grow at every beating—with every type of torture he endured he became more bitter and vengeful—all the while thinking these passionate emotions would make him stronger. Aiden's plan was that his great anger would be the catalyst for his escape— defeating the evil of his father and siblings with the sheer power of his rage.

He would never forget his final visit to the glass room. This time it was a woman who was bound to a chair in the center of the space. Her head was bent and her face obscured by a riot of dark curls. There was something so familiar about her. The scent of the ocean teased his nostrils. He drew in a sharp breath.

"Mother?" he asked weakly.

She raised her head slowly, recognition dawning in her beautiful eyes, "Aiden? My son?"

He rushed to her but was thrown back against the far glass window by the force of Lysha's blue dart. He scrambled to gain his footing. Lysha was standing behind his mother with her hands crushing her windpipe.

"No!" he shouted.

At his scream of desolation, Aiden felt all that was good rush out of him and the darkness envelope his body, mind and soul. He was laser focused on one thing—death. Black tattoos appeared all over his body. They writhed like snakes and turned a gleaming green. His eyes flamed and in his palms blue orbs of electricity ignited. He released every ounce of rage in that one moment and he took his sister's life. Just as his father had planned.

Too late, Aiden realized three very important truths. First, the woman whom he thought was his mother was just an apparition created by his father to goad him into murder. His mother was dead. Second, his sister, unfortunately, was not dead. She had been nothing but an apparition created by his father. Cain would never have put his favorite child, his precious Lysha in harm's way—she was too important to him. And, third, he had failed. Instead of defeating the darkness, his obsession with destroying it with anger had annihilated the Light instead. His rage had been the catalyst for his transformation into a Mescáth. There was no turning back. Aiden understood once the darkness of the night was complete there was nothing more terrifying than the Light.

"Breaking mirrors again I see," Lysha's whiskey-smooth voice jarred Aiden back to the cold reality that was his life now. "Father will not like it. That mirror was his favorite. Picked it up in France in the 1600s I believe."

Aiden glared at his sister in response.

Lysha grinned. "Come on, little brother, let's fix that hand of yours."

Aiden shrugged "It's already started to heal. No big deal."

"That wasn't a suggestion, Aiden," Lysha said quietly. "I know seeing Lily has distracted you. But you must put that aside for the moment. Remember, I made you a promise and I intend on keeping it."

"Ok, sis," Aiden acquiesced. "I trust you."

"Good. I've always had your back, Aiden, and I know you have mine. Now go to the kitchen and get Thomas to bandage your hand. Then meet me in the library. Father has called a family meeting."

"Don't you mean the war room?" he asked sarcastically under his breath.

He made his way toward the back of the house to the kitchen. Thomas, the butler, was up and already brewing coffee.

"Hey, Thomas? Can you fix me up? I ran into some glass upstairs," Aiden explained innocently.

"Hmm, let me guess, a mirror? If I had a face like yours, young man, I think I would look at myself all day," Thomas mused while gathering the first aid kit.

"Yeah, well, I'm not much into my reflection these days."

While Thomas bandaged his hand, Aiden reviewed the events in Ireland knowing his father would want a complete retelling. He would leave out the part about Lily Quinn. It would only anger his father and perhaps make Lily more of a target than she already was. Whatever happened, uniting or not, he would find a way to protect Lily from his father. It was his mission now and he would not fail. Besides, his sister had promised to help him secure Lily's safety. Somehow—someway—he and Lily would have a life together.

CHAPTER 9

Treasures

● ● ●

AIDEN PAUSED OUTSIDE THE ENTRANCE to his father's library affectionately known as the war room. The room's dark paneled walls were littered with the spoils of war throughout the ages: Viking battle axes, Turkish swords, an Egyptian khopesh. Thick Persian rugs covered the floor and heavy drapes hung from the tall windows. Candlelight, the illumination of his father's choice, was the only type of light allowed in the war room. It cast everything in shadow and relief. It also gave Aiden the opportunity to study his family unnoticed.

Lysha, his beautiful yet very deadly sister, was curled up on the couch in front of a roaring fire. She was staring into the flames, a slight smile playing at the corners of her mouth. He wasn't sure what she had to smile about—they had just been soundly defeated in Ireland, losing two Light-bearers. He figured she was imagining the ways she would like to torture a certain Dìonadain warrior. He wasn't sure why, but of all the angels who guarded the Sorcha, Lysha was fixated on Ira.

Aiden figured Lysha was already strategizing her next move against him.

Beside her, lounging in an oversized buttery-soft leather chair, was his father, Flynn Talbot. From across the room, Aiden could feel the raw energy that continuously pulsed through his sire. He so resembled his father, they could have been twins. Not too long ago, Aiden had wanted nothing more than to be like his father in every way possible. But, no longer. His father, if you could call him that, was a cold—demonic—narcissistic murderer. Flynn took a long sip of his customary gin and tonic. Then, he ran his hand over what looked to be an ancient scroll of some sort lying on the coffee table.

The last occupant of the room had been the thorn in Aiden's flesh his whole life—his brother. Kayanja, standing next to a resplendent suit of gothic armor, was the only one who truly looked like he belonged here in the war room. His brother was like a jungle cat, large, elegant and dark, his fury well-controlled—leashed just under the surface of his cool watchful exterior. K was a predatory animal in every sense of the word. Aiden hated his brother and knew the feeling was mutual. The enmity between them ran deep. Growing up, always in competition for their father's love and their sister's attention, Aiden had felt jealousy and anger toward Kayanja. Now, after his cleansing in the Crazies, and the sting of his brother's merciless whip across his back, Aiden felt nothing but cold rage. His brother raised his amber-colored eyes to meet his. Aiden grinned, knowing Kayanja hated his flippant attitude, and sauntered into the room.

"The prodigal son has returned," Aiden announced plopping down beside Lysha. "What did I miss?"

As he had predicted he would, Kayanja exhaled loudly and averted his gaze, showing his disdain for his little brother. Point for Aiden!

"Your sister has already explained the events that transpired in Ireland. I am proud of your tenacity, Aiden. Our loss of two Light-bearers is unfortunate but inconsequential," Flynn stated running his hand again over the leather cords that bound the ancient scroll on the table.

Aiden, relieved there would be no chastisement for Ireland, asked the question he knew his siblings were wondering as well.

"What is that?"

Flynn picked up the scroll and held it gently against his chest, "This scroll is very precious to me to be certain—a treasure. I risked everything to possess it. But, it is so much more than that. It is our guarantee of victory over the Light."

Lysha said, "It looks like it's thousands of years old."

"To be sure," Flynn agreed. "It was written by one of the original Light-bearers and contains great power."

Intrigued, Aiden asked, "How did you get it?"

"Long ago, my dearest children, I was made by Elohim, the Creator of all things, to be a guardian angel. He chose me along with twelve others to serve as defenders of the first Sorcha, Yeshua's disciples of light."

"You were a Dìonadain?" Lysha asked incredulously. "Why have you never told us?"

"It wasn't something you needed to know until now," Flynn answered.

"Tell us everything father," Kayanja pleaded softly.

"I was made guardian to Simon, the Zealot, a master of strategy and warfare in his day, who gave it all up to follow the Light. After Yeshua's death and resurrection, he charged the Sorcha with the task of spreading his light around the world. Simon took his family and traveled to what is now England to preach the message of the Light. While there, he wrote this scroll—the book of Simon. Within it is the secret to the destruction of Abaddon, the darkness and to withstanding any Scáth attack. Simon told me one night what Elohim had inspired him to write."

"What? Is that even possible? The destruction of the Prince of Darkness?" Aiden fired rapidly.

"Can you imagine it? Humans with the power to destroy the supernatural world any time they wish it. I became disillusioned with it all—Elohim, the Light, my duty as a Dìonadain."

"So, what did you do father?"

"I went to Abaddon and told him of Simon's book. Although Simon never told me specifically what the words within it meant, it didn't matter. Both Abaddon and I knew we couldn't let the book fall into the hands of humans. We couldn't let Simon live to write another in its place."

"Why would Elohim give Simon the secret to the destruction of the supernatural world unless his plan all along was for humans to be the real power in this world and the next?" Lysha asked.

"Exactly, my sweet. You too understand the inherent weakness of Elohim—his love for his human creation above all. It's disgusting. I wanted more—deserved more."

"So, what happened next?" Aiden urged.

"Abaddon offered me what I desired so I took it. In exchange for the death of Simon and the end of Sorcha, the Prince of Darkness made me the commander of his demon armies. He placed me in a position that befitted my strength, power and intellect. I took the book the day I killed Simon. Kayanja helped me retrieve it from its hiding place tonight at the museum."

"So, I guess the break-in at the British Museum that's trending all over the news right now was you and K?" Lysha grinned.

"Back when I was creating the persona of Flynn Talbot, I worked for a time at the British Museum. I placed the scroll in one of their vaults for safe-keeping. It seemed the perfect place—I shrouded the scroll in darkness—hidden, forgotten, undetectable—until I had need of it again."

"May I?" Aiden asked. At his father's consent, he unrolled the ancient scroll. "I don't understand these symbols. What does it say?"

"It is all written in some archaic language that I have never been able to decipher. Only the Sorcha can decode Simon's book. I'm not sure how but Abaddon believes they will have the power to do so if they ever unite their powers. This is why we must stop the uniting no matter the cost. Do you understand?"

"Yes, Father," Aiden and his siblings responded.

"How did you kill the Light-bearer?" Kayanja asked quietly.

"There, hanging above the fireplace," Flynn pointed. "I used that saw to cut Simon's body in half in one stroke."

Flynn stood retrieving the saw from its place on the wall. Aiden stared at the saw imagining the horrific murder of Simon at the hands of his father.

"When I sliced into Simon's abdomen, a powerful light exploded from his body. It etched the blade, you see?"

Aiden wanted to study the markings on the saw but thought better of it when his father handed the weapon to Kayanja. If his brother knew he was even remotely interested in the blade, he would move heaven and hell to keep it from him.

"Simon never cried out—no indication of any pain— Elohim's final gift to him I would imagine. He died immediately."

"What was it like? To kill one of the original twelve?" Lysha mused.

Flynn smiled, "A pleasure so sublime, you cannot imagine. I have not felt the like in over two thousand years."

"What do the etchings on the blade mean?" Aiden asked.

"I am not sure. For centuries, I have tried to decode them. I believe they are significant somehow—maybe even to understanding the language in Simon's book but thus far they both remain shrouded in mystery. I feared for a time that the saw was lost to me forever."

"What do you mean? What happened to it?"

"It disappeared the night I murdered Simon. I was distracted for just a moment by the bloodlust of the crowd gathered round.

When I turned back, the saw was gone from the executioner's stone. I learned a valuable lesson that night. Never underestimate the Dìonadain. It was lost to me for many years after that."

"Until the day I killed Eli Quinn, right?" Lysha offered, touching the necklace around her neck that was filled with the Light-bearer's blood.

"What a glorious day it was, my sweet! There it was—just hanging on the wall of Eli's wood shop—hidden in plain sight. Relics are significant to me. Simon was my first kill, and the saw symbolizes my freedom from the Light and Elohim."

"Aren't you worried that someone will take it again, like before?" Aiden asked.

"No, my son. Here—in our home—is the safest place for the saw and the book as well. I want both close to me and protected until we put an end to the Sorcha. We are so very close to having everything we could possibly imagine—endless power and pleasure—forever."

"I don't like it, father," Kayanja urged. "Too many things could go wrong with both your prize possessions in one location."

"Agreed my son," Flynn responded. "That is why I am placing my treasures in your care. Kayanja, you will guard the saw. Simon's book I give to you, Aiden, to protect. My sons—no one is a match for either of you in strength or cunning. You will keep them safe."

"What about me, father?" Lysha asked. "Don't you trust me as much as my brothers?"

"My dear, I trust you beyond all things. You, as commander of my army, will lead the hunt and destroy the Sorcha once and for all," Flynn added.

"Father, I will exterminate them," Lysha added. "There will be no light left in this world when I am done."

"We are finished for now, my children," Flynn announced before he left the room. "Get some rest. I need all three of you at your best for what is to come."

Aiden gently picked up the scroll. Weirdly, the yellowed parchment was warm to the touch. He flexed his fingers in response to the small yet undeniable burning sensation.

"The light within Simon's book must not care for the darkness in you, little brother," Lysha mused. "Where are you gonna hide Daddy's prize?"

"If I told you, I might have to kill you," Aiden teased.

"If you fail, I will kill you," Kayanja threatened quietly.

"Promises, promises," Aiden remarked sarcastically before he spat. "You just worry about protecting that saw, brother."

Aiden exchanged a hard look with Kayanja. Aiden didn't doubt K's intentions but he wasn't afraid. He knew he would kill his brother, one day, maybe soon, who knew? But, Kayanja's death would be by his hand.

"You always were my favorite brother, Aiden," Lysha drawled grabbing his arm after Kayanja left the library. "We will get rid of K together when the time comes."

"It's a deal," Aiden smiled. It felt good, really good, knowing his sister was on his side.

"Keep the scroll safe, little brother," Lysha whispered fiercely. "And stay away from Lily Quinn."

"Your wish is my command," Aiden said earnestly, knowing that was the last thing he was going to do.

• • •

From outside the tall window, she watched.

The dark one took off his white jacket and sat on the edge of an enormous bed.

He ran his large hand across the jagged edges of the saw.

Blood welled on his fingertips.

He raised each finger to his mouth and licked slowly—one by one.

The salty taste must have excited him because his eyes simmered blue.

He took a thick rope of leather and knotted each end.

He attached each end to the saw and slung it across his chest.

He lay down on the bed clutching the saw close and closed his eyes.

She knew this one trusted no one but himself.

The open and close of a door drew her attention.

It was the hothead from the rain carrying a backpack.

She knew the boy must have Simon's scroll in the bag.

Where was he going?

Leaving nothing to chance, she followed the boy.

She caught up with him as he made his way into town.

It was early yet so the streetlights were still on casting a dull glow on the empty streets.

The boy rounded a corner quickly.

He entered a storefront with the name Della's emblazoned on the window.

She moved closer to get a better look.

The boy was talking to an older woman with blonde hair.

The boy handed her the backpack and gave her a big hug.

He ran out of the diner and brushed past her without a second glance.

CHAPTER 10

Messenger

• • •

JUDE PACED THE LAWN UNDERNEATH Lily's window. The rain
had subsided leaving behind soggy grass and heavy mist hanging in the air. Lily's encounter with Aiden a few hours ago had
left him with more questions than answers. Did she still have
feelings for the Mescáth? Would she be resolved in her decision
to keep him at a distance? Had she really forgiven him for his
betrayal? He looked up at Lily's dark window and asked himself the most important question of all. How could he help Lily
understand that any kind of contact with Aiden Talbot was the
worst decision she could ever make for herself and the Sorcha?

He wanted to shout. He was angry. Familiar with the feeling, he recognized he couldn't allow himself to explore the
righteous indignation growing in his spirit because of Aiden's
betrayal and the death of Lily's aunt. He would not interfere.
It wasn't his place to control or manipulate Lily's actions much
less her feelings. The Dìonadain creed was crystal clear.

He recited it under his breath, "The Dìonadain will guard and defend at all costs, never intervening in the life of humanity unless he is called upon or directed by Elohim."

As a Dìonadain, Jude understood Elohim had made him for a purpose. He accepted this truth and embraced it. His sole duty was to protect the Light-bearer, Lily Quinn. He was a guardian defender and warrior of the Light. He was strong, powerful and wise. He could even perform the miraculous, when called upon. But, he could never know the future. It was obscure and remote—beyond his ability to see or his role to comprehend. Only the Creator of all things knew what was to come until the end of the ages. At this moment, however, Jude wished for just a glimpse of Lily's future. He wanted to see the journey ahead so he could prepare for it. He wished to know the danger and heartache that might befall Lily so he could shield her from it.

When Jude saw the blazing coppery light shooting across the twilight sky, he snapped to attention. It was the tell-tale signal of Elohim's chief messenger, the mighty one, Gabriel. Jude swallowed hard and steadied his spirit. He knew there was no way to prepare himself for the sight of this glorious being. No matter how many times Jude had been in Gabriel's presence, he was still overwhelmed with his grandeur. Gabriel was the first among Elohim's angels. He stood in the presence of the Creator and to him were given messages of the highest importance in relation to the kingdom of Elohim. Jude didn't have time to even process the significance of Gabriel's visit before the dazzling messenger landed in front of him with a profound thud.

Jude dropped to his knee bowing his head in deference to Gabriel. Over twelve feet tall, massively built and extraordinarily beautiful, the divine messenger was formidable. Yet, Jude was not afraid. He waited for what he knew would engulf him while in Gabriel's presence—a pure and unadulterated peace.

"Rise my brother," Gabriel bent towards him and said in his soft melodious voice.

Jude grasped arms with Gabriel in greeting and then stood. He continued expectantly, "It is good to see you, Gabriel. You have a message?"

Gabriel's eyes danced in merriment, "Indeed, but, alas it is not for you. Ah, here comes the one I seek."

Jude turned his gaze in the direction of Gabriel's focus. Ira was crossing the yard carrying his charge, Daniel, in his arms. Jude knew the Light-bearer was exhausted. It was no secret Daniel had been praying ceaselessly for weeks, interceding on behalf of his friends, and petitioning Elohim for guidance. Daniel's face was buried in his guardian's wings. When Ira set Daniel on his feet, the Light-bearer dropped to his knees and reached his hands out to touch Gabriel's feet. Jude imagined Daniel was experiencing an overwhelming sense of awe and relief as well as anticipation. His message from Elohim had finally arrived.

"Do not be afraid, Daniel, from the first day you set your humble heart on Elohim and petitioned him for direction, your words were heard. I, Gabriel, Elohim's messenger, have come in response to your plea."

Jude noticed the strength returning to Daniel's body and color to his face at Gabriel's touch. The Believer was being renewed in body and spirit.

"Praise be to Elohim," Daniel stated.

Gabriel bent down to help the Believer stand. "Dear Daniel, I apologize for my delay. I know you have been waiting."

Daniel smiled ruefully, "I admit I was losing hope. I have been seeking Elohim diligently with everything within me for the last twenty-one days. When He remained silent, I was afraid I had been judged unworthy."

"No, Daniel. You have found favor with our Creator. He has not been indifferent to your prayers. I am afraid the fault is mine. You see, the moment you asked for specific understanding from Elohim, He sent me from the heavens to you with a message. Unfortunately, I was detained."

"Detained?" Daniel asked. "What do you mean?"

"Beyond the heavenly gates, outside the protective fortress of the Dìonadain Citadel, the demon called Legion waited. His master, Abaddon, sent him to battle with me. Abaddon's plan was to stop the delivery of Elohim's message or at the very least to delay it so that your heart would be hardened toward our Creator."

"Nothing could turn my heart or my face away from Elohim," Daniel vowed.

Gabriel smiled brilliantly. "I knew it would be so. Your perseverance gave me the time needed to defeat Legion."

"How did you bind him?" Jude asked.

"Oh, he was not bound. His strength was so great he could not be contained. So, we hurled him back down to the earth and into the sea."

"We?" Ira asked. "You didn't face the demon alone?"

"I did, for many days," Gabriel responded. "But, when I failed to subdue him, I asked Elohim for help. Never forget, Ira, Elohim is our strength and our shield. He will never forsake us."

Ira nodded his head in agreement. "What happened next?"

"Elohim answered my prayer," Gabriel smiled. "He sent my brother to help me in my fight. If not for Michael, I would still be battling the beast. Legion is a powerfully cunning adversary. No one else could stand firmly with me in this fight except for Michael. His aid finally provided the breakthrough I needed to get to you now."

The archangel Michael was legendary among the Dìonadain ranks. The chief of angels led them all in skill, strength and combat stratagem. Michael was the defender of Elohim's will and of His people. Despite his possession of unbelievable power, Jude knew Michael to always live his life in total reliance on Elohim. Michael's relationship with the Creator was a beautiful picture of strength and submission. Jude smiled to himself imagining Michael and Gabriel in all their glory flinging Legion into the deep recesses of the ocean.

"Daniel, are you ready to receive Elohim's message?" Gabriel asked.

"I am," Daniel replied.

"Leave us," Gabriel commanded.

Jude followed Ira across the yard. The distance prevented him from hearing any of Gabriel's message to Daniel. As the first orange-hued rays of the sun peeked from behind the house, Jude's thoughts returned to Lily. He vowed to uphold the Dìonadain creed no matter how great his need was to protect Lily from herself.

CHAPTER 11

Gris-gris

• • •

New Orleans, Louisiana

CELESTE ROUSSEAU BOUCHARD WAS LATE to work—again. Bicycling from her home in Faubourg Marigny, one of New Orleans' most colorful neighborhoods, to her aunt's voodoo shop in the French Quarter should have been accomplished in a relatively short span of time considering the distance. But her small detour to pick up what she would need for tonight had taken longer than she had calculated. She would blame it on the rising heat and humidity of the early fall morning and the crazy amount of tourist groups blocking her path as she cycled through Jackson Square. Aunt Delphine would understand— at least she hoped she would.

Celeste patted her jean vest pocket lightly and smiled.

Tonight, she would give the gris-gris, a Voodoo talisman of strength and protection she had created, to her man, Remy Girard. They had met one night a few months ago at The Spotted Cat listening to jazz. Their attraction and connection to each other was instant and they had been inseparable ever since. The fact that he was older than her by five years, tall, dark and dangerously handsome should have put him on her parents' "do not disturb" list right away. However, her father and mother considered Remy's age and looks to be a plus. They were more concerned about Remy's career choice. He had followed in his father's footsteps and become a cop. Remy had just completed his training at the police academy and was now patrolling the streets of the city.

Celeste was proud of her man and wasn't too worried. Surely, Remy's father, the police superintendent, would make sure his son was not put in danger's way. But, just in case, she had fashioned Remy an amulet he could wear around his neck that would protect him wherever he went. She knew Remy would wear the talisman with great pride knowing that he had received a powerful gris-gris fashioned and spelled by a direct descendent of Mariette Rousseau, the Queen of Voodoo, herself. Celeste's storied ancestor reigned supreme over the Quarter in the early 1800's.

Mariette Rousseau, a Creole woman, was considered the most powerful practitioner of voodoo in her day. Placing and removing curses, telling futures, making charms, reading minds and generally serving as a spiritual guide for the masses of New Orleans, Mariette was renowned in life and revered in death. She passed down her secrets to her daughter and her daughter after and so it went until reaching Celeste's mother and aunt and now Celeste, herself. She was proud of her heritage, confident in her power and eager to continue learning Mariette's secrets from her mother and Aunt Delphine.

People have always misunderstood the arts of voodoo, believing them to be evil, dark and twisted. But she knew the religion of her ancestors was rooted in spirituality and the desire to serve others, helping the hungry, the poor and the sick of the community. Celeste had seen people healed of anxiety, depression and loneliness through the charms and rituals that were the hallmark of Louisiana voodoo, just like Mariette Rousseau had done in her reign.

Passing by St. Louis Cathedral and into the heart of the Quarter onto Bourbon Street, Celeste was bombarded by the sights, sounds and smells of her beloved city. She never grew tired of it—the Vieux Carre was an exotic gumbo of attractions and experiences: spicy, sweet, commanding and refined all at the same time. Blending Spanish, French, Creole and American architecture styles together, the Quarter was an enchanting melting pot of design: cast iron balconies, gorgeous ironwork gates, multi-colored buildings, walled courtyards of lush greenery and cascading fountains. It was Celeste's fairytale kingdom.

Checking the time on her watch, she skidded to a stop in front of the store. After locking her bike to the ornate ironwork column that fronted Mariette Rousseau's House of Voodoo, she turned and waved at the old man standing with his trumpet on the corner.

"Mornin', cher, you better get on," an old man urged. "Delphine is waitin'."

Celeste grimaced. "Don't I know it!" She reached up and untied the muted green scarf from around her head letting her thick black hair fall around her shoulders. "Play me a tune, Henri."

"Sure, cher," he grinned putting his trumpet to his thin lips.

Celeste squared her shoulders and prepared herself for the tornado that was her Aunt Delphine. She grinned. People often told her she was just like her aunt——flawless caramel-colored skin, statuesque, and flashing mahogany eyes—but more importantly—brazenly bold, stubbornly confident, and a flair for the theatric. Celeste hoped they were right. She had plans—one day soon she would be sought after like her aunt and her ancestors before her—for her charms, talismans, and spiritual guidance. With Remy at her side, she would reign over the Quarter as its voodoo queen.

But for now, she would work in the store she loved, learn from the aunt she admired, and tonight, she would experience her very first voodoo ritual celebration deep in the bayou. She was thrilled about the secret ceremony because only those selected by her aunt, the reigning voodoo queen, were allowed to attend. She didn't know what to expect because these rituals were shrouded in secrecy and those who took part were sworn to silence. After her initiation, she would give the man she adored her very own gris-gris of protection. She unlocked the door of the shop convinced that today was going to be a fabulous one for Celeste Rousseau Bouchard.

"Bonjou, Tantie Delphine, sorry I'm late," she called in her sweetest voice. "You wouldn't believe the crowds of people out this morning. Crazy tourists are already lined up outside to get in."

When Delphine didn't answer, Celeste walked to the back of the little shop. Mariette Rousseau's House of Voodoo was nothing if not eccentric in its decor and wares. The store served three purposes: a shop filled with kitschy souvenirs and t-shirts for curious tourists, a museum celebrating the history of voodoo in Louisiana and the life of its most famous practitioner, Mariette Rousseau, and a back room where anyone could have their fortune told for a small fee. The shop was a popular destination for many who visited the Crescent City each year. However, unknown to most but available to all was a small room in the basement that could be accessed by those who asked the right questions.

In the secret room, you could request and purchase all variety of medicinal herbs, magical charms, love potions and talismans for money, success, good luck and fortune. As a bonus, everything that came off the shelves in this room was fashioned by the Queen of Voodoo herself, Delphine Rousseau. For a select few, an audience with the queen could be granted where she would foretell the customer's future, far surpassing the reach of the tellers upstairs. Shrouded in secret, she provided guidance to many, no matter their station in life—rich or poor—man or woman. Celeste's aunt was responsible for much of what were the inner workings of New Orleans today.

Celeste figured her aunt was with one of her special clients this morning and that was why she wasn't upstairs in the store. Who knew how long Delphine would be busy? People were crowded at the front door of the store now anxious to get inside and begin shopping all things voodoo. Celeste decided to open the store without her aunt. She just needed to get the key to the lockbox Delphine kept under the front counter. In the lockbox was the specific count of the herbs, charms, and potions they had on hand in the store at any given time. This number changed frequently depending on Delphine's mood and focus as she was responsible for creating said herbs, charms and potions. Delphine liked for Celeste to keep a tally of what was sold each day specifically. She said it helped her connect with what the community's greatest needs were at any given time.

Delphine always wore the key on a thick silver chain around her neck. But because her aunt believed the metal key would interfere with her ability to channel the spirits she relied on in her fortune-telling, she thought it best to remove it when she was meeting with clients in her secret room. The key was kept on a hook right outside the door. Celeste was careful to move quietly down the stairs to the basement so as not to disturb Delphine.

There was the key—right where she knew it would be. Celeste tiptoed to the door and gingerly removed it from its hook on the wall. The door to Delphine's room was slightly ajar. Celeste couldn't help but hear low-pitched voices coming from inside—her aunt's and a man's she didn't recognize. When she peered through the crack in the door and caught a glimpse of the man in the room with Delphine, she felt a sudden chill run up her spine. Her mama had often told her that her chills were premonitions of death or danger to come. She had never given it much thought but right now for the first time she felt like someone had just walked over her grave.

The man was formidable in size. He resembled a statue in the New Orleans Museum of Art so smooth and chiseled were his features. His dark ink skin contrasted with his open-collared white shirt and linen pants. He had beautiful silver piercings in both his ears and his nose. But, it was his unusual amber eyes that mesmerized Celeste. They should have been warm but instead were cold pools of yellow honey. Celeste found herself inching closer to the door, drawn into the man's conversation with Delphine.

"Our preparations are complete," the man soothed. "Your wait is over, cher."

Delphine's cat eyes sparked. "Yes, it will be as it was—as it should be again. My great-great grandmother's dream for her city will finally come to pass."

"Tonight, all of New Orleans will realize the full potential of your power, Delphine."

"Remember, use what I have given you before you begin."

"Are you sure?" her aunt whispered. "I want no mistakes."

A slight smile broke the hardened planes of the man's face. "Use this and all will go as it should."

Celeste wondered at the ornately carved silver flask the man gave Delphine. What was in it? Obviously, it contained something of great power considering the conversation between her aunt and the man. A potion? Gris-gris of some sort? She felt a thrill of anticipation course through her at the thought of the incredible night that lay before her. She had no idea what was going to happen, but there could be no doubt it would be something big.

"Now, I will give you what you need for tonight."

The man moved closer to her aunt so there was only the slightest of space between them. They didn't embrace but Delphine leaned toward him as if he were a magnet. Celeste could almost feel the hum of attraction in the room. She knew she shouldn't remain but couldn't pull herself away from her vantage point. She watched the man remove her aunt's turban. Delphine's hair fell in thick braids around down her shoulders. He placed both his hands on either side of her aunt's face. For the first time, Celeste noticed the dark tattoos on the man's hands and forearms. His amber eyes widened and he began to whisper words Celeste couldn't understand. Delphine's eyes closed and her body began to convulse ever so slightly. The tattoos on the man's hands were glowing a faint green now. When they slid across the man's arms like a snake, Celeste's drew in a sharp breath and moved away from the door. Leaning against the wall, she exhaled slowly. There it was again—the same chill shuddered through her.

"Get a hold of yourself," she whispered under her breath. When she peered back into the room, her aunt was putting her long braids back into her turban. Delphine was alone. The man must have gone out the back door of her aunt's secret room.

"Celeste, child, how long have you been there?" her aunt asked sharply.

Startled, she said the only thing she could, "Just now, I came to get the key when I couldn't find you upstairs. Sorry I was late."

Her aunt stared at her for a long time. Celeste willed herself to return her aunt's gaze with all the innocence possible for a young woman who was lying through her teeth.

"Well, get on with you. Open the shop. You're in charge today. I have much to do for tonight. Close up early. And don't be late, cher. Tonight, is your night."

Delphine breezed past Celeste and disappeared above. Celeste, following orders, opened the shop and then spent most of her day thinking about the mysterious man and watching the clock. The hours ticked slowly by until it was finally time to close the shop. She locked the doors and climbed on her bike anxious for her future. In just a few hours, she would join her family's great spiritual legacy and learn the tradition of secret voodoo ritual. Tonight, would mark the beginning of her real training to someday take her place as the Voodoo Queen of New Orleans. She hardly noticed the people and places she passed weaving through the streets of the French Quarter.

At last! She propped her bike against the garage door of her family home and went in to change. Her parents, Joseph and Clea Bouchard, were already dressed for the night and waiting on her.

Her mother met her at the door and put her hand on Celeste's cheek. "Hurry, bebe, it will be dark soon," Clea urged.

"Yes, ma mere," Celeste answered and kissed Clea's cheek softly.

"We need to be in the bayou before the sun sets," Joseph called.

Celeste laughed, "Yes, papa, I'll be ready in a flash."

She ran up the short flight of stairs to her room. Her clothes for tonight were already laid out on her bed. She quickly undressed and put on the simple shin-length flowing white gown and jammed her feet in a pair of flip-flops. She would be barefoot in the bayou and didn't need anything more. Her mother had made the lovely crimson apron and scarf Celeste would wear tonight with her dress. It was tradition that those who practiced the religion of voodoo would fashion, consecrate and wear beautiful colored aprons and scarves as an homage to the slaves, house workers and hair dressers, like Mariette Rousseau herself, that brought voodoo to New Orleans. She tied the apron on and wrapped her long hair in the soft scarf. Celeste studied her reflection in the mirror. Her eyes sparkled with excitement recognizing the great significance of this night for her and for her family. She was ready!

She took her time walking down the stairs to meet her parents willing her heart to stop racing. Her father had never looked more serious or her mother so proud.

"Tonight, is yours, Celeste," Clea said passionately. "Take it, just like Mariette did. Make it your own. No matter the cost, cher, it will be worth it. It is your destiny."

Celeste nodded her head understanding she would be forever changed after her evening in the bayou. She settled in the backseat of the family Range Rover, the gris-gris she had made for Remy heavy around her neck under her gown, and thought about Mariette Rousseau as the city disappeared behind her.

CHAPTER 12

Fire

• • •

THE LOUISIANA BAYOU WAS BEAUTIFUL yet haunting with its gnarled cypress trees, enormous live oaks, thick palmettos and Spanish moss hanging everywhere like a blanket of grey hair. The dank salty air of the wetlands was still steamy from the hot summer afternoon. As darkness descended, the swamp came alive with creepy-crawly insects, slimy amphibians and deadly reptiles, yet, Celeste thought, there was also an eerie calm engulfing the bayou so vast it felt like it would swallow her whole.

Her parents had walked ahead to join the others already gathering around the shellmound. The mound, largely made up of shellfish, animal and human remains, was an ancient religious site and burial ground constructed by the Native Americans who had once inhabited this place. Thousands of years later, isolated and forgotten, the shellmound still stood in the dense primeval space.

Celeste touched the gris-gris around her neck and thought of Remy. His text messages a moment ago had dampened her mood. It wasn't the fact that Remy had cancelled their date for later tonight because he had been called into work. She understood—he was a cop. It was the reason for the call that upset her. A young boy was missing and an Amber Alert had been issued. The NOLA police were conducting an extensive search for a ten-year-old boy believed to have been taken by someone driving a black sedan. Celeste hoped for the best but knew it would probably be the worst. Not many things made her angry, but adults harming or manhandling kids was definitely at the top of her list. She said a quick prayer for the safety of the boy and for Remy and walked toward the shellmound.

A group of voodoo believers dressed in their ceremonial white, the women with richly hued aprons and scarves and the men with unusual necklaces fashioned of beads, bones, feathers and shells, encircled the shellmound. Torches lit the space creating pockets of alternating fiery glow and deep shadow. Celeste searched the circle for her parents. Her father had taken his place in the ceremonial drumline—her mother was standing in the center on the right of the shell mound. Celeste joined her mother and took her place on the left side. Direct descendants of Mariette Rousseau garnered a special position for tonight's ritual. A silver flask was being passed around the circle—everyone taking a drink. It was the same flask she had seen the man give her aunt earlier that morning. She had been right. It was a potion. When it was passed to her, she lifted it to her lips. The spicy, cloying smell of the liquid inside was very strong. It made her dizzy. When she tipped the flask to drink—it was empty. Not knowing what else to do and nervous she would disrupt the ceremony, she pretended to drink and then passed the empty flask to her mother.

"Open your soul to the spirits, cher, your body to their rhythm. Feel their power rise within you," Clea commanded and then returned to her place on the other side of the mound.

The drums began to beat. Bodies swayed following the rhythm of the drums—dancing with abandon in the flaming glow of the torches. The people started to chant, at first low and then growing loud in a crescendo of unintelligible words. Celeste wondered at everyone around her. They must be feeling something she wasn't. She was frustrated knowing that not drinking the potion was somehow inhibiting her ability to respond. She focused on the drum beat—moving her body—looking to her mother for cues. Clea's eyes were closed as she waved, gyrated, and convulsed in syncopation. Celeste could feel the energy in the circle reaching a fever pitch. Suddenly, the drums stopped.

"The Queen is here," a man shouted reverently from behind Celeste.

Everyone in the circle bowed to the ground. Delphine, regal in her white gown and head scarf paraded around them, slowly stopping in front of the shell mound. Delphine's snake, Zombi, was wrapped around her shoulders, and heavy gold hoops hung from her ears. When Delphine passed by Celeste, Zombi lifted his head and hissed at her. Celeste was unnerved imagining the snake knew she hadn't drunk the ceremonial potion and was not enthralled like the others.

Then, Delphine closed her eye, raised her hands, and lifted her face to the stygian sky. Everyone stared at the queen. Celeste was afraid to breathe. The bayou was still—even the creatures of the night were silenced waiting for the queen to speak.

When Delphine opened her eyes—they were no longer the familiar dark brown Celeste knew—but a fiery red. Her face no longer beautiful but twisted and grotesque. She shouted in a voice not her own, "Bring the child to me!"

Two men, shirtless with tattoos covering their bodies, drug a small wiry boy from the thick palmetto trees into the circle. His hands were bound behind his back. His mouth was gagged and a rope with two leads circled his neck. When the boy struggled or tried to resist, the men would tighten their hold on the leads constricting the rope around the boy's neck even more. The look of terror in the boy's eyes was staggering. Celeste didn't understand what was happening, but she could feel the burning embers of anger ignite deep within her belly. Was this the missing child Remy was searching for? She didn't want to believe that her aunt—her parents—were capable of what she was seeing.

Delphine raised her arms and thundered with authority, "I call upon the spirits of darkness and death. Receive this child—his innocence—our offering to you. Power through fire. Dominion through ashes."

The drums started to beat again. Everyone, including her parents, watched the two men drag the boy up the shell mound. There was a tall wooden pole driven into the top. Short logs of dry rotting timber were stacked against the pole making a platform on the top of the mound. Why hadn't she noticed that before? The men secured the boy to the pole and climbed down. The boy was weeping—struggling to escape—but it was no use. Delphine raised a torch in her hand and ignited the wood stacks under the boy.

"Accept our sacrifice of the innocent," she shouted.

The people screamed with wicked pleasure—convulsing and chanting, attuned to the depravity atop the mound. Smoke curled into the night sky like great grey serpents. The flames were soon roaring climbing higher toward the boy. His head was bent—the smoke so thick around him he probably had passed out.

Celeste didn't think—didn't calculate her best move— she only felt a hot rage boiling within her. She shouted at her mother, her father, anyone who would listen. They all ignored her—their faces and souls no longer their own but belonging to the malevolent darkness pressing in on all sides. Celeste wanted to weep, so desperate and betrayed she felt, but there was no time for that. She had to save the boy. Celeste rushed to the mound and began to climb, ignoring the flames. Two strong hands grasped her ankles and yanked her down the side of the mound. It was Delphine. Celeste rolled over and jumped up to confront the voodoo queen.

"Stop it, this instant! The boy's death will usher in a power you cannot imagine. All will bow to me—to us—the Rousseaus. Remember who you are, Celeste."

"Oh, I know who I am. I am not a murderer. And I am not a Rousseau if this is what it means to be one."

Delphine's crazed eyes flamed a ghastly red. Celeste knew at that instant she was not battling her beloved aunt but a heinous beastly spirit who now resided within her body. Delphine was gone, taken over by the demonic spirit of the voodoo queen.

She snarled and pounced on Celeste like a jungle cat, knocking her to the damp earth. She clawed her face and bit her neck. Celeste struggled with all her might, managing to throw the queen off of her. She had to get to the boy. The flames were hotter and higher now. There wasn't much time. The queen let out a blood-curdling scream and grabbed a flaming torch, hurling it at her. She dodged and took a hard tumble. Something within Celeste exploded. Her entire body raged with righteous fury over the torment of the innocent child. She stood, squared her shoulders and faced the voodoo queen. She had never felt more powerful or resolved than she did at that moment.

"You will not interfere any longer, stupid child," the voodoo queen hissed.

"Silence, evil spirit! You have no power over me. I command you in the name of the innocent to be gone!" Celeste roared—a titanic surge of energy rushed from her soul and exploded like a sonic boom out of her mouth with her final word.

The powerful tide of energy knocked the voodoo queen across the space. She thudded into an oak tree a hundred yards away. Her body convulsed, then was completely still. Zombi writhed on the ground next to his master for a moment and then slid away into the darkness of the bayou. The voodoo worshippers had also fallen to the ground unconscious at Celeste's command.

Celeste had only one thought—the boy. She ran back to the mound. The flames were raging now. She couldn't see the boy any longer the smoke was so thick. But Celeste would not give up. She had to get to him. She started her climb up the burning mound. There was a great boom of thunder and then a torrential downpour. The flames were extinguished, replaced by billows of hot steam. She reached the top and untied the boy. She hoisted his charred body over her shoulder and skidded down the side of the mound to the ground below. The rain stopped.

Cradling the unconscious boy in her arms, the full weight of what had just happened overwhelmed her. Celeste wept, not knowing what to do or where to go. Her tears fell freely wetting the boy's badly burned and unrecognizable face. His hair was completely burned away. His arms and torso were raw and blistered. His legs and feet were so compromised, the flesh was crusted black. He was breathing still but barely—his chest laboring which each effort. Celeste knew he was going to die.

CHAPTER 13

Melee

● ● ●

"Aw, CHER T'BEBE, I'M SO sorry." She closed her eyes and pleaded softly, "Please someone—anyone, help us."

The earth shook under her. She opened her eyes to the most incredible vision she had ever seen. Standing before her was a winged warrior shimmering so brightly that Celeste raised her arm to protect her eyes from the light. Suddenly, the light pulsed and diminished becoming a shimmering, warm golden glow. Celeste opened her eyes again in disbelief. Her eyes accommodated the light, and she realized the winged warrior was a woman—fiercely beautiful, so much it almost hurt to look at her. Her ebony skin was flawless. She wore her hair cropped close to her scalp accentuating the angles of her strong full-lipped face. The elaborately-forged weapon, similar to a sickle, resting heavy on her shoulder was formidable with its scalloped edges and curved tip. Celeste focused on the woman's eyes and immediately felt a sense of peace flow through her. She must have been suffering from shock, she thought, until the warrior angel spoke.

"Do not be afraid, my dearest Celeste, you are no longer alone. I am Imani and I have been sent to help you."

Not understanding but knowing she must, she offered the boy to the warrior angel and responded simply, "Please help him."

Imani bent and took the boy gently from Celeste's arms. Celeste reached out and touched the warrior's massive left wing. It was covered with feathers of the purest white—soft and incandescent. She buried her hand in the deep thickness wanting to feel and know that what she was seeing was not her imagination but something real.

She looked up at Imani in confusion.

Imani smiled slightly and nodded her head, somehow understanding Celeste's need for tangible proof.

The warrior laid the boy gently on the ground and said over her shoulder, "Zoe, it is your time. See to the boy. I will set a perimeter."

Imani walked away a short distance—drew her gleaming gold broadsword from the scabbard at her hip and drove into the ground. A shimmering barrier, humming with electricity, enclosed them on all sides. Celeste watched as Imani brandished the sickle shaped blade again and took a ready stance for battle.

The boy's labored breathing drew Celeste's attention away from the winged warrior. A lanky red-haired girl was sitting cross-legged on the ground beside him—holding his hand. This must be the Zoe that Imani had summoned. Celeste couldn't imagine what this girl could do for the boy. Surely, he only had moments before he left this world.

"You saved him, Celeste. Now, the power of the Light will make him whole," Zoe promised earnestly before turning back to the boy.

Celeste watched as Zoe ran her hands over the entire length of the boy's body—back and forth. Her head was bent, and she was whispering the phrase "in the name of Elohim" all the while. Celeste held her breath, unbelieving, as the burns on the boy's body began to fade and disappear altogether. What she was witnessing wasn't even possible let alone logical. But it was happening nonetheless. The boy's breathing became stronger as his wounds healed. When he opened his eyes, Celeste just shook her head in wonder.

"Celeste, come here, someone wants to meet you," Zoe beckoned.

Celeste crawled over to the boy who was now sitting up. His clothes were tattered and charred but his body was whole and without blemish. When she felt the boy's tight hug, she accepted completely that everything that had happened tonight was very real.

"You're gonna break me, little one," she said softly. Pulling back from his embrace, she asked, "What's your name, cher?"

"Paul, my name is Paul Thibedeaux."

"Well it's very nice to meet you Paul Thibedeaux. You are going to be just fine, I promise."

"Celeste, I want you to meet my friends, Daniel and Wei," Zoe gestured. "We all came for you."

For the first time, Celeste noticed the rest of the small group gathered around her. There was a dark-haired young man about her age kneeling close by, his hands folded in a position of prayer. Beside him an Asian girl wearing a New York Yankees baseball cap keenly studied their surroundings. Celeste bet not much got by this one. She seemed vigilant yet perfectly calm—an interesting combination. Her hand rested lightly on the young man's shoulder in prayer.

Behind them and along Imani's forcefield were three more glorious winged warriors. The first was a dark male who carried a huge oaken shield with gold and silver rivets making the sign of a cross across its broad expanse. He held a gleaming broadsword that could have cut a person in two without much effort. The second, also a male, was pale with spiky white-blond hair. He twirled two pointed, lethally sharp pronged weapons in his hands while his ocean-blue eyes were trained above on the dark sky.

But it was the third warrior, a woman who rivaled Imani in both beauty, stature and presence that unnerved Celeste. She pulled a bow from her back and a quiver of arrows. She thrust the arrows in the ground beside her. Training her eyes on the space outside the perimeter, she drew her bow back locked and ready. When the warrior turned her head and met Celeste's gaze, she was taken aback by the strength and power that rested in her grey eyes. What battles must this warrior have fought to earn such a gaze?

"Agatha is quite magnificent," Zoe remarked. "All the Dìonadain are really."

Celeste couldn't help but agree. But what or who were the Dìonadain? Who was Zoe and the other two with her? Had they been there all the time? Obviously, they had come with Imani. But how had they gotten there? Why were they here— in the bayou—at a secret voodoo ritual?

"You came for me? But, how did you know where I was?" Celeste asked.

"Daniel found you. Elohim sent him a message," Zoe said brightly.

A white sizzling clap of lightning across the black sky changed the atmosphere within Imani's forcefield and prohibited any further explanation from Zoe. The winged warriors immediately tensed and moved to defensive positions around Celeste and the others.

"The Scáth are here," Imani warned, glancing quickly at the blond warrior. "We need to move, Tov."

"Zoe, get the boy," Tov ordered. "Ira, shield!"

"Behind me!" the dark warrior with the mammoth shield shouted.

Celeste helped Zoe pick Paul up and stand him on his feet. They held him between them and rushed to join the others behind the oaken shield.

"Just there," Agatha aimed her arrow. "Through the trees, here they come."

Celeste was dumbfounded as she watched hundreds of silver lights rush at them through the trees. Breaking the tree line, the lights shifted and became extraordinary winged creatures clothed in gleaming silver. Their leather wings were translucent, and blood pulsed through them. Some wore masks, others did not, but all had fiery crimson hair, glowing green tattoos writhing on their bodies and eyes burning with cold blue flame. Whirling around and above Celeste, the Scáths bombarded the forcefield with blue flaming darts. There was no longer any doubt for Celeste about who the good and bad guys were. She was seeing a battle between good and evil right before her eyes.

Celeste had always believed in the supernatural— the voodoo religion recognized the existence and power of the spirit world. She had built her life around this knowledge. But, she now knew what she had believed all her life about the goodness of voodoo and its power to help people had all been a lie. The spirits and powers of her ancestors—of her family—were not grounded in good but in evil. The golden warriors who protected her, Zoe and her friends who helped her, they were fighting on the right side of things, and that's where Celeste wanted to be.

"Too many of them," Ira shouted. "We need to leave, now!"

"Agreed," Imani responded.

"Agatha and I will hold them back," Tov said twirling his swords in his hands.

"Make it so," Imani shouted.

Imani pulled Celeste under her left wing and Zoe under her right. Her wings folded around them creating a cocoon. Ira picked up Paul in his arms and wrapped his wings around Daniel and Wei.

"Ready!" Ira thundered.

"Eyes on me, Celeste," Imani urged.

She should have been scared out of her mind but she wasn't. She didn't know why but Celeste trusted Imani. She buried her hands in Imani's thick wings and squeezed tightly.

"Now," Agatha shouted.

Imani withdrew her sword from the ground and the force-field disappeared. Immediately, Agatha's arrows sliced through the demon melee. When her golden arrow made contact with a Scáth, it was bound in a molten cord of gold. Tov, alongside her, deflected Scáth darts meant for Agatha, with his sai swords. Meanwhile, Imani and Ira shot up into the night sky in a shower of light, carrying their charges with them. Celeste held on tightly as they rocketed across the sky, the bayou disappearing behind them.

CHAPTER 14

Choices

● ● ●

IN ONLY MOMENTS, THEY LANDED softly. Imani's wings unfolded from around her and lowered her to the ground. The grass felt cool under her feet. The ruins of a grand plantation house stood off in the distance, the moon casting an ethereal glow around it. Paul ran to Celeste and grabbed her hand. Celeste could only imagine what he must be thinking after their ordeal. She was shaken to her core.

"We will be safe here while we wait on the others," Imani said quietly. "Ira?"

The dark warrior nodded his assent and moved away into the shadows.

Celeste sat down, Paul beside her. Zoe and her friends joined her to wait. They seemed nonplussed by all that had just taken place—as if it were a common or a natural event. Zoe and Daniel were chatting quietly while Wei was eating a candy bar she had taken from her jacket pocket. Celeste shook her head slightly—she had so many questions.

"Oh, my goodness, Celeste, your hands," Zoe said.

Celeste looked down at her hands—red and blistered—noticing for the first time that she was burned and she was in pain.

"It must have happened when I was climbing the mound."

Zoe reached over and took Celeste's burned hands in her own.

"In the name of Elohim," Zoe spoke with quiet authority.

Celeste felt a wash of warm liquid heat course through her, starting in her hands. Before her eyes, her wounds began to heal. After a few moments, her skin was smooth, clear and undamaged once again. She touched her neck where the voodoo queen had bitten her, then her face, which had been covered in deep angry scratches, and found no injury. Celeste was incredulous. She stared at Zoe in wonder.

"How did you do that? Who are you?" she asked. "I need someone to explain to me what's going on."

"It's actually a lot simpler than you think," Zoe answered with a solemn smile. "The God of all creation, Elohim, has had his eyes on you since before you were born, Celeste. He instilled within you a special gift. An incredible power he wants you to use for good just like you did tonight."

"I don't understand. A power?"

"You felt something out there when you confronted the queen that you've never felt before, didn't you? Like a switch flipped—a trigger was pulled—and bam!—a door flung open releasing a tremendous wave of warm energy through your body, mind and soul—all at the same time. You felt powerful—no fear—only that you had to save the boy?" Zoe asked, moving her hands excitedly as she talked.

"Yes, exactly. The energy focused me—empowered me. I didn't have to think—I just knew what to do."

"That was the power of the Light you felt coursing through you, Celeste. Your gift from Elohim was ignited because of your righteous anger about what was happening to the innocent boy," Wei said.

"Wei is right," Daniel added. "Elohim has given you the ability, in the name of good—the Light—to cast the darkness and evil spirits out of people at your command. You wield a very powerful gift. Even in the midst of all the chaos you feel right now and all the unbelievable things you have witnessed, you still feel a sense of peace, yes?"

"I do, at least a little. It's so strange, like I'm in the eye of the storm raging all-around me."

"Yes, the calm you feel, the power you exercised tonight, it is the Light, Celeste," Zoe said.

"The Light?"

Zoe continued, "Elohim's son, Yeshua walked this earth thousands of years ago with a mission to save the world. He did and that's why we are all here now."

"I'm familiar with Elohim and his son Yeshua. Remy told me about God and his son Jesus. I even went to church with Remy a few times and heard stories about them. They are one and the same, yes?"

"Absolutely. But since the beginning, they have been known as Elohim and Yeshua," Zoe agreed.

"I always thought it was just a story—a really good story—but fantasy nonetheless. After the things I have witnessed tonight, I can only believe that the stories were the truth. My family has practiced voodoo for hundreds of years so I have always known about the supernatural—but I was seeing it from the wrong perspective. What I knew to be the power of voodoo was actually the power of evil. A battle between light and darkness, demons and angels, miracles and curses, it's all very real."

"Real to everyone who will just open their hearts and minds to the truth," Daniel said quietly.

"But how can it be that Elohim would give me this great power to use for his purpose if I am descended from a long line of voodoo queens, followers of evil. I don't understand?"

"You are a descendant of one of the twelve, the first Light-bearers. Yeshua chose twelve men, his disciples, to bear and wield his holy light here on earth for good. There is a great movement of evil in this world, and it is our purpose to fight and destroy it," Zoe encouraged.

"How do you know for sure that I am one of these Light-bearers?"

"Behind your ear, you bear the sign of the Sorcha, just like we do," Wei said gesturing to her ear.

Celeste reached behind her ear to find a small raised pattern, tender to the touch. She had noticed a burning sensation back in the bayou that had lessened to a slight sting now. She figured it was just a burn from the flames at the mound.

Zoe turned her head exposing her mark. The moon illuminated a small design that looked like a twelve-pronged star.

"The sign of the Sorcha," Zoe said. "When a Light-bearer's gift emerges, the sign becomes visible."

"What are your gifts?" Celeste asked.

"Wei is the Wielder. She used her gift to change the course of nature tonight. She made it rain so you could rescue our little friend here. We don't go anywhere without Daniel. He is the Believer. His prayers make our guardians stronger and faster when he seeks Elohim. You will meet the others soon."

"And you?"

Zoe laughed. "Well, I'm the Healer. I thought that was pretty obvious."

Celeste returned her laughter but then asked the question that had been stirring in her while they had talked.

"Zoe, I want what you, Daniel, and Wei have. I want the Light to always shine in me. I want to fight the darkness I witnessed tonight. How can I be sure that I am worthy of the Light?"

"None of us are worthy, Celeste. We don't deserve the great gifts Elohim has given us," Zoe answered.

"But, he chose us—you—for this mission. We only have to accept his call and fight for the Light," Daniel added.

Celeste knew she wanted to live the rest of her life fighting for the Light—for all that was good and true. She wanted to step away from her past and into her future as a Light-bearer.

"Daniel, will you pray for me? Will you ask Elohim to accept me?"

"I will pray with you, Celeste, we all will. But you can ask him yourself," Daniel responded kindly.

Celeste joined hands with the strangers around her, although she already felt like they would be her family. All four bowed their heads. Daniel led at first, but then he squeezed Celeste's hand for her to pray.

When her prayer was finished, Celeste knew her life had been changed forever. She couldn't wait to learn more, be more and do more. She was a Light-bearer and she had a battle to fight in the name of the Light.

"Celeste?" a man's voice called in the distance.

She knew that voice. It was Remy. But how did he know where she was?

"Over here, Remy," she answered searching the dark for him.

She stood when Remy pushed through the palmetto bushes. He was alone. She ran toward him wanting to get to him before he saw Imani, knowing he would surely flip when he saw the supernatural warrior. But her winged protector wasn't there.

Remy grabbed her and hugged her close. "Celeste, are you ok? What are you doing out here?"

"I'm fine. I have so much to tell you, Remy. But how did you find me?"

"I was searching this area for the boy that's missing. I ran into a man about a mile back. He said he had heard voices around the old Dubois Plantation and thought maybe I should take a look. Who are they?" Remy asked, pointing to the others still sitting on the ground.

"Friends, good people, Remy," Celeste promised. "We found the boy. Look, here he is. Paul, come here," Celeste called.

The boy came and stood beside her looking up at her for reassurance.

"This man is my friend, Paul. His name is Remy, and he is going to take you home," Celeste encouraged.

Remy crouched down to get eye-level with Paul.

"Are you hurt, Paul? Can you tell me what happened to you?"

"Yes sir. I'm ok—just still a little scared. Some very bad voodoo people took me and tried to burn me alive. But Celeste saved me. She got me away from them."

Remy looked at Celeste wanting answers. But Celeste knew now wasn't the time or the place. Who knew how long they had before the demons from the bayou would find them.

"Please take him home, Remy," Celeste pleaded. "A few miles that way back through the bayou, you will find a shell-mound. My aunt, my parents and others are there. They're the ones who took Paul. They were going to burn him alive as a sacrifice tonight. I didn't know, Remy. Please believe me."

"I believe you, cher," Remy assured caressing her face. "I will have to arrest them, you know. I'm sorry."

"I'm not." Celeste shook her head. "They lied to me—all my life—they betrayed me. They are evil people, Remy. They should be punished for what they tried to do."

"Let me take you home—all of you. We will get this sorted out," Remy promised.

"I can't go with you, Remy. Not now. Listen, I can't explain it all right now but I have to go away for a while."

"What are you talking about Celeste? You aren't making any sense," Remy answered.

She took both his hands in hers and squeezed them reassuringly. "There is so much I want to tell you, my love—so much I need to share. But there is something I need to do—something very important that can't wait. Please know I am safe and that I will be back as soon as I can. I need you to trust me, Remy."

Celeste met Remy's gaze steadily, willing him to see her deep love for him and her promise that she would return. He must have seen it, because he nodded his head and squeezed her hands back before dropping them.

"Paul, buddy, I'm gonna take you home. Your parents have been worried sick about you."

Paul's mouth widened in a big-toothed grin. "Yes sir, I'm ready."

Remy leaned into Celeste and kissed her softly on her forehead. "Don't keep me waiting long, cher. I might just have to come find you."

And with that, Remy and Paul, hand-in-hand, walked back into the dense trees at the edge of the plantation. Celeste watched until she could no longer see the pair.

When she turned around, Imani stood behind her glowing in the dark night. The other warriors had joined them and were standing with Zoe, Daniel and Wei.

"I'm proud of your strength and wisdom, Celeste. That was a difficult thing you just did. Come with me now. Your destiny awaits you."

Celeste, never one to shy away from a challenge, moved confidently into the shadow of Imani's wings.

"Let's go," she urged, pulling the gris-gris from around her neck and throwing it on the ground. "I'm ready to be who I was meant to be."

In a flash, the Light-bearers and their guardians disappeared, leaving the bayou very far behind.

CHAPTER 15

Memories

• • •

Lost in thought, Zoe sat on a wooden pew in the old church. Candles flickered gently around the sanctuary. Zoe sighed. It had been an eventful evening to say the least. They had all made it back to Centenary safely. She liked Celeste—she had more personality in her little finger than most people did in their entire body! She was fearless and Zoe admired that very much. Her heart was joyful knowing that she had played a small part in helping Celeste accepted the call of the Light on her life.

She knew the others were either downstairs getting to know Celeste or already back at the house getting ready for one of Aunt Audrey's big suppers. It was game night tonight! Zoe loved the competition and rampant humor that always accompanied one of these nights with her family and all her new friends. They might be sequestered, safe within the protective boundaries of Centenary, but that didn't mean they couldn't have fun!

Counting the colored pieces of stained glass in the windows had become a pastime for Zoe. It helped her to think and sort out what was bothering her from time to time. Most days, she was a sunny-side up sort of girl. But, lately, she had been wrestling with questions from her past. Tonight, had crystallized something in her. She needed answers—that was abundantly clear. Seeing that little boy, Paul, knowing he was frightened to death, struggling to understand what had happened to him, only triggered thoughts about her own past.

The heavy iron doors creaked open in the back of the church. Soft steady footsteps sounded on the wooden floor. She didn't have to turn around to know who it was.

"Beni, can we talk?"

"Zoe, you know I'm always here for you," Beni said warmly. "I got worried when you weren't at the house so I came looking."

"And you knew where I'd be?"

"Of course," he grinned and slid in beside her. "What's up?"

'You know when I told you I wanted to know more about my real mom and dad?"

"Yeah, I remember," Beni said. "But, Zoe, we both decided there was no way to find out what you want to know. It happened so long ago and there were no witnesses."

"I know, but, I think I figured out a way to deal with the impossible."

"Zoe, Beni, what are you two doing here? You are supposed to be back the house with the others," Tov chided.

"I know. But, I'm not breaking any rules. I asked Nolan if I could wait here for you. Besides, Beni is here and Asher is right outside."

"There is no winning with you, is there?" Tov remarked good-naturedly.

"Not when she's made up her mind about something," Beni added.

"This is serious, Tov. I need you to do something for me—and you aren't going to like it."

Tov's demeanor changed immediately, "What is troubling you, Zoe?"

"Will you sit with me?" Zoe patted the space beside her.

"Certainly," he responded.

"Tonight, seeing that little boy and how confused and frightened he was, it really got to me, ya know?"

"I can understand that—seeing others in pain or experiencing fear is difficult. Go on," Tov encouraged.

"Well, it got me thinking. I mean I've always wondered and hoped one day I would find out. But, we've been kinda busy lately so it's been in the back of my mind. Now, though, it's something I really need to know."

Tov laid his hand gently on hers to calm her. "What is it you need to know? I'm listening."

"I need to know about my parents—my real parents. I deserve the truth," Zoe demanded. "And I know you can show me?"

"It will be painful for you, Zoe," Tov countered.

"Pain that will make me stronger. I need to know who I am. Surely, I have memories of that night. I was there."

"Please, Tov, help her unlock the memories," Beni pleaded for his friend.

"I know you can, Tov. Rafe told me the Dìonadain can show someone the past."

"As you wish," he said. Tov, a being of few words, ironic since he was matched with her, nodded and placed his hands on either side of her face.

"You are the worst singer in the history of singers," Rachel laughed.

It was Christmas, her husband Josh's favorite holiday of the year, and that meant Christmas carols—all the time. Josh had been singing at the top of his lungs since they had left the church holiday program heading home.

"I definitely am, but the best way to spread Christmas cheer is singing loud for all to hear!" Josh answered with a big smile.

"Zoe will never fall asleep with all your racket," Rachel teased.

"Zoe loves to hear her daddy sing, don't ya, baby girl?" Josh nodded toward the back seat where his 2-year-old daughter was strapped into her car seat clapping her hands.

Josh and Rachel McCant had been married four years before they welcomed their red-headed bundle of joy into their sweet family. Zoe was a delight—always smiling and full of curiosity. Rachel reached back and grabbed Zoe's foot and squeezed it lightly.

"Who wants cookies when we get home?"

Zoe giggled with glee.

"And hot chocolate!" Josh added.

Rachel rubbed her stomach softly knowing that tonight would be the most special Christmas Eve ever. She would tell Josh and Zoe the wonderful news! This time next year, they would have a new little McCant to celebrate the holidays with.

"The snow is really coming down, now," Rachel remarked. "We should have left sooner."

"Reggie needed my help, babe," Josh replied. "It's tough being the only pastor around for miles. He would have been there all night cleaning up if we hadn't stayed."

"I know, you're right. But, it sure is lonely out here. I haven't seen another car at all."

"It's ok, just the bridge to cross and we're home."

Be careful, Josh, the roads are slick. It will be even worse when we cross the bridge."

"I'll slow it down."

"I never thought I would say this, but, would you sing another song?"

Josh laughed and started booming The Twelve Days of Christmas.

Rachel relaxed and sang along. They would be home soon, in their pjs, celebrating in just a few minutes. In a split second, the unthinkable happened.

The dark green SUV veered right. With no way to control what happened next, Rachel watched everything happen in slow motion. She opened her mouth to scream, but there was no sound. Josh's eyes never left the road. He gripped the wheel and tried to keep the vehicle on the dark icy bridge. But the front wheel caught the edge of the bridge's concrete wall. The vehicle flipped in the air suspended for a moment before crashing into the icy waters of the Spanish Fork river. They landed upside down in the shallows with such force the windshield exploded and blew out of its frame. The roof of the car was crushed like an *aluminum can. Rachel tried to get her bearings. Zoe whimpered in the back seat.*

Water rushed in through the gaping hole the windshield had left. Rachel, still strapped in the passenger seat, couldn't move. She was sure both legs and at least one arm was broken. A tremendous pain shot up her neck when she tried to move her head. From the corner of her eye, she saw Josh. His face was smashed. There was blood everywhere.

"Josh, talk to me," she wept urgently. "Please Josh wake up. Help me."

Rachel took her good arm and reached for Josh's hand. She squeezed it but he didn't squeeze back. Somehow, she knew he was already gone. The water continued to fill the car. Her curly red hair was now soaking in the quickly rising water. She didn't have much time. Zoe continued to whimper softly in the backseat. Rachel couldn't see her but figured she was still strapped in her car seat.

"It's ok, baby girl. Mama's here. Let's sing a song ok? On the first day of Christmas, my true love gave to me..."

Zoe quieted down.

As the water covered her eyes and nose, Rachel prayed, "Lord, please save my baby, or at least let her go to sleep so she doesn't suffer," Rachel whispered before she took her last breath.

Zoe opened her eyes and looked at her protector. She knew the peace she was feeling regarding her memories of that night was because of him. Tov smiled gently and removed his hands from Zoe's face.

"What caused my father to swerve, Tov?"

"It remains a mystery, but luckily you were found in time. Out of sight from the road, the SUV sat in chest-high foaming water for twelve hours before it was discovered by some fishermen. They called 911 and then dashed into the water—it was so cold they had to be treated for hypothermia later."

"How did they get me out of the car?"

Tov continued, "Your rescuers turned your parents' vehicle on to its side and discovered you in the backseat, alive. You were upside down and strapped into your car seat. It kept you out of the water and your clothes dry. You were suspended there just above the churning river—sleeping like a baby should."

"Just like my mama prayed for," Zoe whispered with a slight smile. "But, how did I come to be with the Quinns?"

"Your father was a distant cousin to Mia and her sisters. When there were no other relatives that could be reached, the authorities called Mia. She and Eli came to Utah immediately and took you home. You were their daughter from first sight. Never doubt it!"

"I don't. I know they love me—Lucas and Lily too. But, why not tell me?"

"Would it have made a difference?"

Zoe thought for a moment and then cocked her head with a grin, "Not in the least. May I ask one more question?"

Tov nodded his head.

"Was the accident that killed my parents an attack of the enemy?"

"Why would you think that?" Tov replied with his own question.

Beni interjected, "It makes sense. The Scáths caused the accident killing Zoe's parents because they were afraid about who they might become in the future or what they might do to fight the darkness?

"But, Zoe lived, didn't she? You see, Abaddon and his minions know nothing of the future. They only operate in the here and now. If they had known who Zoe was they would have never allowed her to live. Zoe's parents died tragically, yes, and we have to accept that it was their time to leave this world. But, they live on in Zoe and in all the people's lives they touched while they were here."

"Thank you, Tov, for trusting me to handle to truth," Zoe said.

For the first time in a very long time, she didn't wonder anymore. She knew who she was. She knew where she was going and she was thankful. She felt a familiar hand in hers.

"You ready? Let me walk you home," Beni said.

"Can we take the long way? I just want to be outside for a while," Zoe said.

"A lot to process? I get it," Beni said.

Hand-in-hand, they left the chapel. Quietly, slowly, they made their way through the rose garden, by the dancing fountain and across the quad. The trees were awash with the golden and red colors of fall. When they arrived at the house, Jack, her happy lab, bounded down the front steps to greet them.

"You know why I'm not sad?" Zoe asked suddenly while rubbing Jack's ear.

"Tell me," Beni urged.

"Cause it's even more clear now that Elohim had a plan for me. Knowing that there is so much going on around us that I can't see or even understand, I know that I know that He is watching over me and He always has!"

"That's what I had to keep telling myself after Alvaro died. And even now, I wonder if I will ever be truly happy again without him," Beni added.

"Beni, here's the truth. It doesn't matter what happens to us—to any of us. Our circumstances don't mean we can't choose to be joyful. When you realize that even the bad stuff is working for your good, it's a lot easier to have faith even when it hurts."

"I'm glad I got you, Zoe," Beni said. "I wouldn't be able to handle any of this without you."

"I'm glad we have each other," Zoe smiled and kissed him on the cheek. "Come on in, I smell dinner!"

CHAPTER 16

Pink Stuff

• • •

DeFuniak Springs, Florida

Lost in her music, Harper Grierson hadn't noticed the passage of time or the darkening sky. A sudden clap of lightning startled her. She reached for her cell. It was as dead as four o'clock on a Sunday afternoon in DeFuniak Springs. Her hometown, located on Florida's panhandle coast, was a quiet community—Harper's translation—boring times one thousand. She couldn't wait to graduate from high school—just one more year. She loved home but she had big plans. Her heart was set on attending Centenary College in Tennessee. The school's stellar music program and close distance to Nashville made it perfect for Harper.

Harper smiled thinking about how funny life was. Hers had ended up taking some crazy turns. She had played sports all her life. In fact, she had promised to attend a Division I university on a basketball scholarship. In the 10th grade, she led her team to win state as the star center. The great thing about basketball is that people appreciate your height and strength unlike the world outside of the arena. Harper quickly learned that when she blew out her knee right before her junior season. Without basketball, days turned to months laying on the couch feeling useless. She struggled to find purpose until she was asked to participate in the worship band at her church as a backup singer. Harper had never considered herself a singer. In fact, she had never sung at all, but when she held her first piece of music, everything changed. She taught herself to play the guitar, and as the days of playing and singing melted into weeks and months, Harper found her true joy in life. It was a different kind than she was used to for sure. No longer was her happiness dependent on how well she performed on the court or the screams of the fans in the stands. Harper was saturated daily in the joy that comes from singing praises to whom she believed was the Savior, and soon enough, she transitioned into a soloist. She now dreamed of standing and singing on the Grand Ole Opry stage. A music degree, some serious training, and hopefully a few good connections would bring her closer to making her dream a reality.

Well, maybe if she survived her mom's reprimand. Harper's ears were already blistering just thinking about the chastisement she would get when she walked through the front door of her family's farmhouse! Even without knowing the exact time, Harper knew she was late—beyond late. She was sure her mom had sent multiple text messages and called several times already. Her mom was nothing if not predictable. She probably had Harper's dad out looking for her now. Her mom always thought the worst, especially since Jolene Tucker had disappeared several months ago.

The sweet and friendly people of DeFuniak Springs, Harper's parents included, had become cautious and maybe just a bit paranoid wondering what had happened to Jolene and who might be the next to disappear into thin air. There was talk among the congregation that Jolene might have been kidnapped or even murdered. But Harper didn't buy it. She had grown up with Jolene. The girl had always been trouble. She had never gotten along with her parents, had probably just run away, fed up with small town living and looking for the big lights in the city.

It didn't matter what Harper thought though. Whenever she left the house now, she would get a long speech from her mom about the dangers of girls being out alone and how the world isn't a safe place anymore. Today was no exception. Harper had promised her mom, like always, that she would only practice with her band a couple of hours, that she wouldn't be by herself, and she would come straight home after.

But in true Harper fashion, band practice had ignited her creative energies. She had decided to stay behind, despite her friends' invite for burgers and shakes at the diner. She wanted to get the chord progressions and lyrics spinning in her head down on paper. Ever since she had worked up the nerve to sing at the local coffee shop on open mic night and received such a positive response, she couldn't stop writing, perfecting and performing. She had worried that she wasn't pretty enough with her long unruly brown hair, fair skin and full figure—or even talented enough, but if the views she was getting on her videos were any indication, people liked her and her music. To date, she had uploaded three songs and shared with her growing audience about her inspiration and how important music was to her soul and spirit.

Even though her parents didn't like her posting videos on the Internet, much less chatting with strangers, they were passionate supporters of Harper's dream to be a musician. However, their enthusiasm did not include a free pass for tardiness or for what they would consider a lack of responsibility on her part for letting her phone die. At least, she figured, she wasn't breaking all the rules. She wasn't alone. Purlis, the old custodian at the church, was somewhere in the building cleaning for Sunday service. She had seen his dilapidated green truck parked out front earlier.

She gently laid her guitar in its case and snapped it shut.

"A storm's comin'," a gravelly voice said from behind her.

She turned quickly to find Purlis Kanaster standing a few feet behind her leaning against a door frame with a broom in his gnarled hand. Purlis was a peculiar-looking man. In fact, people often said Purlis looked like he had seen ten miles of bad road. His head was sparsely populated with wiry white hair, his teeth were yellowed and chipped and his tanned face was drawn with lines of age. But his physique was hard, lean even, from years of labor in the hot Florida sun. He was quiet. Harper guessed she had only ever heard him say a few words in all the time she had known him, but Purlis always had a warm smile on his face, ready to help anyone in need.

"It don't look good out there," he mused with a frown. "You better get on home, Harper."

"Yeah, I was just going," she answered, picking up her case.

Purlis moved away from the door frame, put down the broom and stepped closer. His scent engulfed her. It was horrible—sweet and sour all at the same time—it reminded her of elementary school and the awful smell of fresh vomit and the pink powder stuff the custodian sprinkled on the mess before cleaning it up. Harper held her breath and tried not to grimace.

"I'll walk you out—make sure you get in your car, ok?"

"Nah, I'm fine. No worries."

But then, Purlis stepped in front of her and tried to take her hand. Harper felt the little hairs on the back of her neck prickle. She was nervous. But why? Even though he was acting a little strange, Purlis was harmless. The storm and worry about being late just had her spooked.

Harper shoved her hand in the pocket of her jeans and pulled out her phone. "Better call my mom and let her know I'm on my way." She moved past him deliberately and made her way to the door.

Over her shoulder, she exclaimed, "See ya Purlis. Gotta go. My dad is probably already out looking for me."

Purlis nodded, a faint smile curling his thin lips. "Alrighty then, but, you best be careful, Harper. This storm has been brewing a long time. It's gonna be a doozy."

Harper breathed a sigh of relief when Purlis turned away and walked to the back of the church. She was being silly—he was a harmless old man. She guessed her mother's warnings earlier had gotten to her more than she realized. She was just a little uneasy and hyper-sensitive, that's all. Another sharp clap of lightning and she quickly flung open the wooden front door. There was Purlis. He was just sitting casually on the front steps of the church looking up at the dark sky. She was amazed she hadn't tripped over him. How had he beaten her outside from the back of the church? Something was wrong.

She felt the first wave of real anxiousness then. The little voice inside her head told her to turn around, go back into the church and bolt the door. But her car was just a few feet away. She could make it—she wanted to get home. She ran down the steps toward her car.

"I don't reckon you gonna beat that storm now, Harper," Purlis said quietly.

Harper understood what Purlis meant when she saw the two men coming for her. Her adrenaline spiked—her only thought survival. She screamed instinctively. The country church was at the end of a long drive, far from the road, not that anyone would be driving by to hear her anyway. But, she screamed nonetheless. Her mama's worst fear was now Harper's cruel reality.

The skinny one closed in first. Her mom's words of advice, ridiculous to Harper at the time, came back loud and clear— "elbows, knees and nails, baby girl—fight till you ain't got no more fight left." The skinny one wrenched her arm pulling her roughly into him. She dug her nails into his stubbly face, scraping flesh. He released her arm.

She spun around and ran for her car. Big burly arms grabbed her from behind. With all her strength, she jabbed her elbow into the man's midsection. He loosened his hold but only slightly. But it was enough. She was tall and stronger than she looked. Harper spun around and drove her knee hard into her assailant's groin. Again, she was free. Her car was so close.

The paralyzing shock of the Taser probe in her back dropped her immediately, painfully, to the ground. Her muscles cramped and spasmed horrifically—fifty thousand volts of electricity coursed through her body. Harper gasped for breath—helpless and unable to move. Thick silver duct tape was placed over her mouth. Her ankles and hands were bound. She was unceremoniously tossed into the back of a dark van. It all happened in just a few seconds. Her world had changed in an instant. She wished she had listened to her mom.

The sickening smell surrounded her again. It was Purlis— the harmless old custodian who had fooled them all. He bent low over her and drew in her smell deeply like an animal sniffing his prey.

"I been patient, Harper, waitin' for you." He picked up a strand of her curly hair and rubbed it across his ugly face. "You're so much sweeter than that crazy Jolene."

Harper felt bile rise from her stomach into her mouth. All the time, it had been him. Jolene hadn't run away. Purlis had done something awful to her. Now, he was going to do the same or worse to her.

"Remove your hands from her," a woman hissed from the front seat.

Harper watched Purlis' face go white and his eyes narrowed. He moved away at the woman's command. Deciding she needed to memorize everything she saw and heard just in case she survived this, Harper studied the woman's profile. Obviously, she was in charge and Purlis was scared of her. The woman was exotic-looking. Her long black hair hung in a thick braid across her shoulder. She was dressed in a fitted leather jacket. She was definitely not from Defuniak Springs. But, Harper was most disconcerted by the woman's eyes. They were a startling shade of blue—almost glowing in the dim light of the enclosed vehicle. Before Harper could wonder anymore about the woman, she felt a hard pinch and everything faded to black.

CHAPTER 17

Chains

• • •

Harper moaned weakly and opened her blue-grey eyes. She surveyed the darkened room. Small—no windows—a steel door—concrete walls and floor—a meager light attached to an overhead fan was slowly spinning above. Two empty cots stood against the cold walls of her stark cell. Her head was pounding ferociously. When she tried to move from the thin mattress she was lying on, spasms of pain shot through her. Her quick indrawn breath paralyzed her with revulsion. The same sickly-sweet aroma assaulted her senses, and memories flooded back—Purlis, his dirty cloying odor, the guttural voices of the horrifying men—accents she didn't recognize, the painful rigidity of her cramped muscles as the taser volts pulsed through her body, the sour bile in her mouth.

So stupid! So weak! She had been overpowered in a moment. Her attempts to resist had been futile considering the strength and speed of her captors. She had been bound, gagged and thrown into the back of the SUV within seconds. The sudden pinch of the cold needle in her arm had left her with this insidious headache and dry mouth. She needed water. She needed to clear her head if she was going to figure a way out of her current situation.

She pushed herself up to sit, but when she tried to swing her legs off he cot, she realized her right ankle was shackled to a thick iron chain fitted into the center of the concrete floor. She was confined and restrained like an animal. Her breath came shallow and quick—a tremendous weight pressed down on her chest. She was going to have a panic attack—and it was going to be a monster!

Her first attack had come during the Christmas holidays when she was ten years old. Home from school, she was playing hide and seek with her two older brothers. Wanting to finally win for a change, she had hidden herself in a small closet in the family basement, confident her arrogant brothers would never find her. Unfortunately, she had been wrong. Not only had they found her hiding place, but, being mischievous and wanting to have some fun, they had locked the door from the outside, trapping her inside. It was hours before her father had found her curled into a fetal position, whimpering and shaking all over. Ever since, she had been afraid of small, dark spaces.

She had to get out of this room. She jumped up from the cot and went to the center of the room. She tugged hard on the thick chain that bound her. Unyielding, it clanked on the hard floor. She screamed in frustration—her pulse racing now, nausea roiling in her stomach. No matter how much she struggled she couldn't release herself. Minutes ticked slowly by—nothing changed.

She sunk hopelessly to the cold floor, her energy spent. She beat her fists against the thick impenetrable concrete and hung her head. Just like Jolene, she was going to die here, or worse, she would be used, tortured, unspeakable things done to her body and to her soul—things too horrific to speak of or to think about. She knew what happened to girls taken by the kind of men who had abducted her. She had heard the stories—in the news, in school assemblies, and horror movies. Instinctively she knew real life could be so much worse than anything she had ever imagined. She pressed her face into the unforgiving floor, closed her eyes tightly, and whimpered like a child.

"Please Elohim, I don't want to die. Please, save me. I feel so alone."

Her eyes widened when she felt a small hand squeeze hers.

"Don't be scared. I'm here."

Harper lifted her head and looked into a pair of large dark brown eyes. They belonged to a small girl who couldn't have been more than ten years old. Harper had noticed the empty cots before but must have missed the small occupants who must have been hiding underneath them. From her vantage point lying on the floor, she could make out the form of another girl below a cot on the far side of the room.

The little girl with the brown eyes squeezed her hand again. She instinctively scooted closer. Inches separated them, eye to eye, Harper felt the girl's sweet breath on her face. The girl looked at her curiously and then smiled solemnly. The moment passed quickly but Harper felt an instant connection to the dark-haired, fair-skinned child.

"I'm Cora. That's Sarah," the child pointed. "She's real scared. She hasn't said anything since she's been here. But, I told her we have some time before the men come back. They haven't given us anything to eat yet so they won't come back till after that," she chattered normally. Her little voice had a bizarre calming effect on Harper in spite of her very dire circumstance. Again, Harper felt drawn to this child.

"What's your name?" Cora asked, twirling Harper's hair around her finger.

"Harper," she answered, startled her voice sounded so strong. The crashing waves of panic were gone. She felt calmer, more in control. If this little girl could do it, then so could she. She smiled at Cora, squeezing her little hand.

"Come on, Sarah," Cora beckoned. "Come meet Harper."

At Cora's insistence, Sarah crawled slowly from the darkness beneath her cot. The thick chain around her ankle clinked loudly as she moved closer. She had a wild look in her dark eyes. Harper understood. She knew she must have had the same look in her own eyes moments before. Sarah's pale eyes were bloodshot. Her bottom lip was swollen and there was a slight bruise on her left temple. Harper figured Sarah to be about thirteen or fourteen years old.

"See Sarah, I told you an angel was coming to help us. And now here she is. You are going to save us, aren't you Harper?" Cora asked confidently.

A strong wave of emotion washed over Harper. She wrapped the girls in her arms and pulled them close. "I will do whatever it takes. We are gonna get out of here, girls, I promise."

Trapped, chained, no control over their situation, Harper waited with her two small charges. She had no clue how she was going to make good on her promise. But she knew she had to be strong for them. She would protect them. Elohim had answered her prayer. She wasn't alone. Granted, the girls weren't exactly what she had been thinking of in terms of help from Elohim. But she trusted that Elohim knew what she needed better than she did herself. She needed something to ground her, to take her focus off of her panic and put it toward surviving. The girls' need for a protector provided that for her. They needed to know that someone older was going to watch over them and take care of them. She was their answer to prayer. Harper smiled thinking about the mysterious ways of Elohim. She was no angel but she would defend these two girls as if they were her own blood—her family. Let them believe she was angel, if that thought gave them hope then so be it. She prayed quietly, the two girls sleeping in her arms. She stared at the steel door and prayed for courage and strength to face whatever or whoever might come through next.

Harper had no idea how much time had passed. She awoke with a start when the lock on the steel door clicked loudly. The heavy door swung open. It was Purlis and behind him two very large men dressed in black. She looked directly at him willing herself to show no fear. What Harper had once thought was an old man's sweet smile was now a predator's evil grin.

"Which one of you pretty girls are going to dance for the master tonight?" Purlis asked.

Harper met his hot gaze defiantly. Her worst fear was confirmed. Sarah trembled in her arms. Cora must have scurried under the cot when the door opened because she was gone. She was glad the little one was out of sight. Maybe they would forget she was even in the room. Harper squeezed Sarah tightly, willing her to be strong. Like thousands of young girls and boys across the country every day, they were being trafficked, sold like animals into sex slavery—forever lost from their homes and families.

"That one," Purlis said softly pointing to Sarah but never taking his eyes from Harper.

Harper tightened her grip on the whimpering Sarah and shielded her with her body, "No, please," she begged. "Please, Purlis, you can have me."

Purlis chuckled. "Now, that's a fact, Harper. I will have you. But not tonight."

He motioned to the men, "Get her on outta here. He's waiting." Her plea fell on deaf ears. Sarah hid her face in Harper's shoulder.

Sarah wailed, speaking for the first time, "Please Harper, save me! I don't wanna go. Please don't let them take me."

Harper held the sobbing girl but wasn't strong enough to keep the two men from taking Sarah from her. Purlis unlocked the thick chain from Sarah's ankle. Harper watched in horror while one of the men bound Sarah's hands and then her feet. Sarah no longer struggled but seemed to be in some catatonic state. The other man picked her up and tossed her over his beefy shoulder, carrying her from the cell.

When Purlis turned to follow, Harper grabbed his arm, "No, wait."

He crouched down beside her and studied her intently.

She grabbed his leathery arm and whispered urgently. "Purlis, don't do this. Whatever you want, I'll do it. Just please don't hurt Sarah."

He grabbed her chin and brought her face close to his. Her stomach roiled in reaction to his foul breath. She willed herself to be still, to not be repulsed by him. When he rubbed his lips over her face and in her hair, she felt like she would vomit. She started trembling.

"Soon, Harper, real soon, you and I are gonna dance," Purlis whispered hotly in her ear.

He let her go abruptly and moved to the steel door. Two different men entered the room then, dressed in the same black as the others. One carried a girl who was no more than twelve while the other a little boy the same age as Cora—both were unconscious. The men dropped their packages roughly on the cots and attached thick ankle chains to each one before leaving the room and locking the heavy steel door.

Harper, still trembling from her encounter with Purlis, knew there wasn't much hope that Sarah would ever return. She was grieved imagining the horrors that awaited the girl outside their cold cell.

"I didn't save her," she whispered. "Sarah is gone and we are all lost forever."

Harper was crushed. The little girl had trusted her to protect them and she had failed. She turned away from Cora and crawled back to her cot. She was absolutely still.

The room was deathly quiet. The other children were still unconscious, sleeping off the intravenous cocktail delivered by their captors. Harper was alone with her thoughts, her fears, her questions. Her mind was swirling fighting against her fear, her panic, her failure, and her horrific reality. She did the only thing she could. She started to sing—softly.

"Be Thou my Vision, O Lord of my heart
Naught be all else to me, save that Thou art
Thou my best Thought, by day or by night
Waking or sleeping, Thy presence my light."

As the song rose from her heart, her voice grew stronger.

"Riches I heed not, nor man's empty praise
Thou mine Inheritance, now and always
Thou and Thou only, first in my heart
High King of Heaven, my Treasure Thou art"

The boy and the girl across the room from her were awake now, listening. They stared at her in wonder. She knew they must think her crazy. Maybe she was, but she didn't stop. She couldn't. The music was humming through her entire body now. She had to let it out. She had to sing. Her mind and spirit focused solely on the song, her favorite hymn. Somehow, she knew even if she didn't survive this, it was all going to be okay. She reached behind her ear to scratch a dull burning itch. Something so small and insignificant, but it gave her courage. She was still alive. There was still hope. When the two new-comers left their cots, and joined her sitting on the floor, she held their hands tightly. They smiled and Harper sang louder.

"High King of Heaven, my victory won
May I reach Heaven's joys, O bright Heav'n's Sun
Heart of my own heart, whate'er befall
Still be my Vision, O Ruler of all."

Suddenly, there was a great rumbling beneath her and the floor shook violently. It must be an earthquake, she thought. The children screamed. The light flickered off in the room plunging it into total darkness. Harper sat with both children pulled against her trying to protect them. They were gasping and shaking with fright. She didn't feel much better. There wasn't much they could do chained to the floor and huddled in the dark. It was surprisingly silent. She wondered about everyone else near them. Surely, they would come check on them. Or maybe they were all dead. And even now, Harper and the children were buried beneath rubble and lost to the outside world. She raised her head and opened her eyes. A blinding light burst from across the room. She covered her eyes.

"Do not be afraid, Harper." a gentle voice urged.

She opened her eyes again to see a magnificent woman standing before her in an ethereal glow of gold and white. It was Cora but yet, not Cora. This woman was older; she was what Cora would have become in twenty years. She was wearing form-fitting gold armor that pulsed with light. She had a massive sword strapped to her hip. Her feet were encased in silvery grey boots. Her long dark hair fell in waves around her shoulders. Two braids interwoven with silver rings formed a crown on her head. Her features were so perfect and yet so soft. And folded behind her back were a pair of what could only be described as wings—full, feathered, wings!

Harper knew she had to be dreaming. This just wasn't possible. But warrior Cora's eyes were child Cora's eyes, warm, gentle, peaceful. She dared a quick look away from the glowing warrior to see if Cora was in fact still lying under the cot across from her. She wasn't surprised to see the empty space.

"It is as you know it is, young Harper. I thought a younger version of myself would be best for you at first. I have been appointed as your guardian—your protector. Elohim has sent me."

"I don't understand."

Cora smiled. "Elohim put a new song in your mouth today, Harper, a song of praise. Many will see and fear, and put their trust in Elohim because of what happened here. These little ones will have a story to tell." She pointed to the chains that bound Harper and the children.

Harper gasped when she saw that the thick iron chains had fallen off.

"It's time to go Harper," Cora urged. "Take their hands. Don't let go."

"What about Sarah?" Harper urged. "We can't just leave her here."

"No, we most certainly will not," Cora replied. And with that she was out the steel door.

"No matter what you see or what happens, don't let go of my hand," Harper ordered. "Got it?"

Both children nodded. A low rumble shook the cell again—the strong vibrations caused plaster to crumble and fall from the ceiling. They needed to get out of there fast before the entire structure fell on their heads. Harper led the children beyond the steel door into a dimly lit hall. Fluorescent lights were swinging haphazardly above. Where plaster had fallen from the ceiling, steel beams were exposed. Doors to other rooms hung ajar on their frames. Stress-fractures ran along the walls and the concrete floor was buckled in places.

Cora stood in the middle of a long hallway but she wasn't alone. There was a male dressed in the same golden armor as Cora carrying a mammoth machete. He was undoubtedly the largest man she had ever seen—his muscles had muscles. Beside him was another man, older than Harper but young still, well-built with thoughtful green eyes and a thick dark beard. She sensed his steadfast resolve and courage but also a hint of sorrow, she was drawn to him immediately.

"Harper, meet Makaio, a guardian like myself, and this is Ioan. They are both here to help us," Cora explained.

Harper gazed steadily at Ioan but he paid her no mind at all. He was studying the crumbling walls. Yet, another vibration shook the ground and a large section of plaster toppled from the wall.

Ioan grabbed her arm roughly and pulled her back, the heavy debris just missing her. He released her so quickly Harper wouldn't have believed it had happened at all except she could still feel the imprint of his strong hand on her arm.

Ioan shouted, "Gotta move, Cora!"

"Go, Ioan, lead the way." Cora ordered.

Ioan ran down the hall. Makaio followed him holding the other girl from the cell in his arms.

Cora nudged Harper and said. "Bring the boy."

Harper picked up the little boy and held him close. "Hold on little man."

Harper ran down the crumbling hall after Cora. Every man and woman Harper passed along the way was standing or sitting frozen in place—except for their eyes—obviously very aware but with no power to move or respond. Harper guessed they were stuck in whatever position they had been in at the time of the quake. She knew every single one of them would be trapped in the building when it fell.

"There, Harper," Cora pointed. "Up those stairs. I'm right behind you."

A metal staircase loomed large at the end of the hall. Makaio was there waiting—his golden arm reaching for her. She hugged the boy tight and ran toward the stairs.

A forceful vibration shuddered beneath her. She stopped to steady herself. A thunderous crash sounded overhead. Harper looked up to see a steel beam coming right for her. Instinctively she shielded the boy and waited for the monstrous slam that would end her life. But it never came. She looked up. Ioan was there—every muscle straining—crouching beneath the tremendous weight of the steel beam he held on his back. He met her eyes—his full of purpose.

Harper just knelt there motionless—she couldn't believe what she was seeing. No human being could hold that weight.

"Harper," he roared. "I can't hold this forever, move!"

Before she could obey, Cora swooped behind her carrying her and the boy she still held in her arms to the metal stairs. Harper looked back over her shoulder for Ioan. He stood lifting the beam over his head. With another roar, Ioan tossed the beam. It landed with a great thud. Makaio was there and helped Ioan to the stairs. He was ok. He had saved her. Who was this guy?

Still holding the boy, Harper climbed to the top of the staircase, another heavy steel door blocked their way to freedom. Cora touched the tip of her glowing sword to the lock and it melted away instantly.

"Right behind me, do not waver," Cora commanded.

Harper nodded, understanding whatever lay behind this door would be the most perilous part of their escape. Cora, sword at the ready, pushed the door open easily with her foot. Harper put the little boy down, took his hand and followed Cora outside. Ioan led the girl out with Makaio bringing up the rear.

The evening breeze was light upon Harper's skin. The full moon beamed in the night sky. Armed guards lined the colonnade of the sprawling Spanish-style hacienda, their bodies frozen just like the ones downstairs. The guards' eyes tracked them as they traversed the cool marble floor.

Harper eyes widened. It was Purlis. He was incapacitated like the others, seated and leaning back against one of the thick marble columns. His mouth was open—his tongue hanging out grotesquely. His short shallow breaths communicated his anger and helplessness.

She knelt down by him looking him dead in the eye. Harper muttered, "I guess you won't be getting that dance after all, Purlis. My friends here will make sure of that."

His eyes widened at her words, taking in the glowing warriors behind her. They were fearsome to behold. Purlis' only response was a gurgle deep in his throat. Harper breathed a sigh of relief knowing that this awful man would never be able to hurt her or anyone else ever again. She moved away from him giving him no other thought but pity. Harper smiled, listening to the rhythmic roll of the waves on the shore that must be on the other side of the mansion. They were free.

When Cora halted in the middle of the marble passage, her stance aware but not defensive, Harper knew the warrior was waiting for something or someone. Harper instinctively drew back when a tall dark young man approached them from the shadowy trees at the side of the house.

'Do not be afraid," Cora said gently. "He is with us."

But Harper had already figured that out when Ioan quickly embraced the dark man.

"Everything is as it should be. I believe you need me now, Cora," the young man said gravely.

"Yes, Daniel. It is time," Cora replied. "Ira?"

"Here, Cora," said a male standing just at the edge of the tree line. Before Harper's eyes, the man transformed from a normal guy into a golden warrior just like Cora and Makaio. "Daniel and I were detained—a little party in the bayou."

"You were successful?" Cora asked. "She is safe?"

"Yes, the Exiler is safe at Centenary now," Daniel answered. He turned to Harper and introduced himself. "I'm Daniel Barzani, a friend. You have been very brave, Harper. Elohim is guiding our steps. We will be home soon."

For a quick moment, Harper studied the stranger beside her. Older than her, but not by much. She wasn't sure but his accented speech and sharp swarthy features surely marked him as a foreigner.

Her head swirling with questions, Harper put them aside and continued down the marble hall with the others. Cora, in the lead, halted at the center of the long colonnade. There was a bridge, lined with sculptures of frighteningly life-like deep-sea creatures, an octopus, a dragonfish, and a frilled shark. It led across the grotto pool that surrounded the house to a small torch-lit patio. Men were sitting around the area in cushioned lounge chairs. At the center of the space, was someone Harper would never forget. It was her exotic dark-haired kidnapper. The evil woman was tightly holding a girl from behind and held a wicked looking knife to her throat. The girl's eyes bored into Harper's, screaming silently for help.

"Sarah!" Harper yelled.

Harper let go of the boy's hand and ran to the bridge. She stopped dead in her tracks when Cora moved swiftly in front of her and plunged her glowing sword into the ground. Harper felt the force of energy that circled from the sword and completely surrounded her and the children. She extended her hand toward it and felt its strong vibration.

"We can't leave her," Harper pleaded.

"We won't," Cora answered. "Hold fast," she commanded. "The Mescáth is mine."

The Dìonadain warrior pulled two long daggers from the leather sheaths attached to her sinewy legs. Harper was amazed. It wasn't difficult to understand what would happen if struck by either of the two intimidating weapons. In Cora's right hand was a dagger of fire while in her left was a dagger of ice. Cora brandished her fire and ice daggers in the air and moved across the bridge deliberately, her massive wings spread wide. Harper didn't understand it, but for some reason the evil woman holding Sarah was not frozen like the rest. And for that matter, she had absolutely no fear or shock on her face at the sight of the glowing warrior coming toward her. In fact, she looked almost thrilled. Her full lips spread into a cold smile. Her blue eyes pulsed with light.

"Let the child go, Keket," Cora ordered quietly.

"She matters not, Cora," Keket replied drawing the blade ever so slightly across Sarah's exposed throat. Harper cried out when she saw the blood ooze from the girl's neck. Her body fell lifeless to the patio. Sarah was gone. She had never even had a chance. Harper pushed on the invisible shield around her but couldn't break its bond. Helpless to change the horrifying reality in front of her, she watched helplessly as Keket stepped over Sarah's body like it was a dead animal. Cora's gargantuan wings beat the air around her. Her body glowed hot. Harper had never seen a look so fierce as the one on her warrior defender's face.

"I didn't know what I had taken. Thought she was no one like all the others. Brought her here and I didn't even know who she was—until now. And you think I'm going to let you take her from me!" Keket screamed. "The Believer may have the power to disable everyone here through his prayers to your master, but, I am Keket, the darkness before midnight."

Keket and Cora met at the center of the bridge in a flash of color. Blue flames shot from Keket's hands and eyes. While, Cora deflected each with her fire and ice daggers. It was a warrior dance as old as time. Harper knew that Keket had been talking about her. She didn't understand what it all meant but she knew the fight taking place in front of her was about her, for her, and because of her. She prayed for Cora's strength and for the golden warrior to win.

She turned to Daniel who was kneeling beside her. His hands and arms were extended. His voice was strong, insistent and commanding, as he prayed for the warrior in the fray before him. Cora's armor glowed hotter and brighter as Daniel prayed. Ioan, holding both of the children closely now in his strong arms, studied the fight intensely. Makaio and Ira both stood at the ready waiting if Cora needed them.

Keket was agile and skilled but could not subdue the golden warrior. When Cora gashed Keket's arm with the fire dagger, the Mescáth screamed in agony—the scent of burning flesh filled the thick air. But Keket was a fierce fighter. She catapulted over Cora trying to get the advantage from behind her. Harper gasped. Blue flames shot from the evil creature's hands and coiled tightly around Cora's neck. Keket laughed with delight as she tightened the chokehold on the angel's neck. Cora strained against the pulsing blue coils.

Daniel began shouting his prayers. With each word, Harper could see renewed strength in her guardian angel. Cora flexed her neck muscles and broke the blue restraints imprisoning her. She shot up in the sky, her mighty wings thundering in the air. When she dove back toward Keket plunging her daggers into the Mescáth's chest, Keket dropped to her knees. She was immobilized. Harper figured Cora's weapons, combined with the power of Daniel's prayers, were too great for Keket to fight off. The cold blue flames in her eyes were enough to let Harper know, Keket wouldn't be down for long.

Cora yanked her daggers from Keket's chest and ran back towards them. She withdrew her sword from the ground releasing the invisible shield around them. The warrior reached down to help Daniel from his kneeling position. The young man, sweat beaded on his brow, smiled ever so slightly and said, "It will hold, Cora, do not worry."

"I don't doubt it, Daniel, I wish to have you, the Believer, always at my back, praying for my advantage," Cora replied and then turned her attention to Harper. "I know you are grieved for Sarah. But she is with Elohim now, free and home."

"I know, but I wish she hadn't died all the same. What happens now, Cora?" Harper asked.

"Now, we leave this place. It's time for you to know who you are, Harper."

Harper didn't have time to fully process Cora's words, before the warrior wrapped her arms tightly around her and they shot up along with the others into the sky in a radiant rainbow of light.

CHAPTER 18

Gehenna

• • •

"I HAVE FAILED YOU, FATHER," Keket sank to her knees, her head bent low to the ground.

In the past twenty-four hours, she had been duped, not once but twice. Without advance modes of detection, two Light-bearers had emerged and escaped her and her Scáth spies. One had even been in her possession, and she had had no clue about her importance. Everything had gone miserably awry. Keket feared her father's wrath. Her inability to gain him his prize not once but twice would not go well for her. Her body tensed, anticipating the beating she knew she would likely receive, even if she was his favorite. Time was running out as they moved closer and closer to the uniting of the light that would destroy them.

"You, my beloved one, could never fail me," Cain soothed. Her father reached out and touched her face. His large and well-manicured hand was cold. "But I fear we both will have some explaining to do."

"He summoned us both?" Keket asked, dread and excitement warring within her. "I am going with you? to Gehenna?"

"Yes, my sweet, the master would see us both," Cain answered with a faint smile. "I fear you will not like it very much."

"No, father, I think not," Keket agreed. "But it is only a temporary domain just until our master comes into his kingdom."

"The Kingdom we are supposed to secure for him? Yes, certainly," Cain responded. "Steel yourself, my sweet, Gehenna is a cold and cruel place."

Her father spread his dark wings, and she stepped into their embrace.

"We are going to Israel, yes?" Keket asked.

"The Valley of Gehinnom in Jerusalem has been thought by many to be the gate to Gehenna. Children were once sacrificed in pagan ceremonies there, making it a foul and evil place. But, alas, the gate is not there. The entrance to Gehenna can be found anywhere in the world. Ingenious really! Whenever it is needed, the gate will open and swallow whatever is standing there like a black hole."

"Spectacular," Keket breathed in awe. "I'm ready father."

"*Si vocare infernum,*" Cain declared.

Keket's shoulders had barely sunk below the level of the ground before all light was obliterated. Within the shelter of her father's wings, she shivered. Day and night just blended into one another here in Gehenna, the kingdom of Abaddon. Blackness came with such completeness, Keket wasn't sure she still even had eyes. The darkness was as thick as the wall of an ancient city. It was a land whose light was darkness, a pit of gloom and disarray. The air was rife with the stench of sulfur; she knew the smell must be from the lake of blue fire that surrounded and ran through the city of Gehenna. Her father had told her of the lake—its blue flames didn't consume. They just kept on licking coldly, delivering punishment and pain for whomever was cursed to spend their eternity there.

When Cain landed softly and unfurled his great wings, Keket had her first glimpse of Gehenna. She studied her surroundings. The ground beneath her feet was dry and unforgiving. In front of her, towering twelve feet tall, was a colossal gate made of dry stone. Flanking the gate were two menacing Scáths, clad in silver armor and swords drawn. Their fiery crimson hair, flaming blue eyes, and translucent leather wings pulsing with red blood reminded Keket of the incredible strength and power of these dark creatures. They bowed their heads in deference to her father.

The snake-like tattoos on her arms started to writhe and gleam green. Keket smiled to herself. The Scáths of her father's army were already under her command. One day, very soon, when she had stopped the uniting, the legions of Scáths that made Gehenna their home would all bow to her as well. At least, that was her prince's plan, one her father knew nothing about. Abaddon had been visiting her room in the Talbot mansion in secret for months now. Abaddon was displeased with her father. He knew of Cain's plan for his Mescáth bloodline. Instead of stopping Cain, however, Abaddon had decided he could profit from it instead. He had promised that Keket would rule at his side—his consort—his queen—when he came into his kingdom and defeated Elohim once and for all by destroying the Sorcha if she would destroy her father in turn.

In the distance, the city rose from the ground. The burning flames from the lake cast the city in an eerie blue glow. It was the only illumination in the obsidian dark of the underworld. The desperate screams of tortured human beings echoed everywhere.

"You'll get used to it," Cain said, reading her thoughts. "Poor souls, they actually believed choosing our Prince over Elohim would bring them wealth, health and happiness. Ironic. He doesn't want or need them. Humans are beneath him and us for that matter. Pawns in a deadly game. Their destruction is a strategy to undermine the purpose of the Light and nothing more."

"What do you mean, father?"

"Abaddon's only goal is to make Elohim's creation hate their Creator. He wants to dethrone Elohim in humanity's heart and mind. Our Prince wants to make Elohim appear cold, unforgiving, evil and malevolent. When something bad or awful happens to a human, especially one who believes in Elohim's Light and sovereignty, he sees the pain, destruction or loss as Elohim's punishment, or worse, a lack of provision, protection or love. He will blame Elohim for his misfortune."

"So, humans are angry at Elohim. They turn away from him. They allow evil to take root in their hearts and turn to our Master instead."

"Exactly. The more human lives Abaddon acquires, the more powerful he gets and the more he destroys Elohim's greatest love, humankind. Come, my sweet, you must see this," Cain beckoned.

Keket followed her father through the daunting gate. Waiting on the other side was a Scáth holding the reins of two snarling black beasts with razor-sharp teeth. They were large, their bodies covered by coarse hair, and silver leashes gleamed around their thick necks. She mounted her beast and followed her father into the city across a bridge spanning the lake of fire. Ravens circled above them. Sounds of human agony became louder as they got closer to the city. Here she was, in Gehenna, the city of darkness, the pit of hell, and she had never been happier to be anyplace in this world. They reigned in their beasts, and she watched with sick pleasure the sights of suffering around her.

"Behold, the fiery lake of Gehenna in all its glory and wonder," Cain said proudly.

The endless burning lake was roiling with the thrashings of all who had been sent there throughout the ages of time. Some floated, moaning with a pain so deep and wide, it resonated in the space like a bass drum, while others bobbed up and down in the fiery water with mouths gaping in soundless agonizing screams. Keket's green tattoos continued to writhe across her exposed arms, seeming to draw energy from the suffering of others.

"Look! There!" Cain pointed.

A hundred yards away, a human was swimming toward the bank of the lake. Two others followed behind him, struggling and obviously desperate to escape the torture of the water. The first human clawed up the dry sandy bank of the lake into the horrible mixture of briars and nettles that scattered the surface. The ravens overhead began to caw hysterically. Keket watched with pleasure, anticipating what would happen next. Suffering in Gehenna is eternal, so she knew there would be no escape for the humans. She didn't have to wait for long. The sand on the bank of the river moved, signaling the advance of one of the terrifying beasts that made Gehenna their home. Her father had told her of the giant serpents and locusts that guarded the shore of the city. Which one would climb from the depths of the sand?

The ravens shrieked when a wicked black locust climbed from below the sand. It was the size of a horse and wore an armored breastplate. The locust had the face of a man. Long black hair hung from its head. A dull golden crown sat atop its massive head. Completing the terror of this hellish beast was a long, curved tail with a wicked stinger at the tip like a scorpion. The human screamed in terror and attempted to run across the sand, but the locust was too quick. It covered the distance in one powerful jump using its back legs. Grabbing the human in its razor-sharp front legs the locust whipped its curved tail over its back and drove its stinger into the human's flesh. The venom paralyzed the human. Keket watched the man's eyes roll back into his head. The locust dropped his prey to the sand. In seconds, the human's body convulsed sharply and exploded into four large pieces.

"I don't understand, father," she shouted. "The human is dead?"

Cain smiled back at her, "Wait for it."

Swooping down from the dark sky, they came—four demon Scáths. A dry foul wind stirred the sand around the fallen human. The locust crawled back down into the depths from which it came. Swords glinting silver, each demon stabbed a part of the human's body and raised it overhead. When their swords pulsed with blue flame, the Scáths joined their swords piecing the human's body back together again with the power of the blue flame. Consciousness was immediate—the human's horrifying scream rent the cold air. As the human's body was catapulted back into the lake of fire, the other two humans were suffering a similar fate a few yards down the lakeside.

"Superb!" Keket exclaimed.

"What is true suffering? Boundless pain? Unending torment? Mindless agony? Yes, of course. But the true genius of inflicting everlasting suffering is reminding the human of that which he will be without forever."

"I see. The human is allowed to escape because he fears living another day of this life—and then to die—but only for a moment. Yet, in that minuscule second in time the human experiences a release from eternal torment. It's a moment of peace—the sweet reward of death. But, then in a flash it's gone, and the torture returns only to be felt in greater agony this time. The human will suffer more because he is reminded in that second of oblivion of what it was like to hope."

"Poetic, isn't it?" Cain suggested.

"And deliciously beautiful," Keket agreed.

"Our Prince is waiting, my sweet," Cain announced. "He is angry with us to be sure. But he also knows we are the only hope he has of stopping the uniting. Do not be alarmed. I will handle things."

"Of course, father, I will follow your lead," she replied.

Keket's allegiance was no longer with Cain but with her Prince. She knew she would do whatever she must to secure her position in Abaddon's kingdom, even if that meant betraying her father.

Perfection

● ● ●

ENTERING GEHENNA, KEKET MARVELED AT the ancient walled city. The majestic sound of a classical symphony filled the city streets. Abaddon was known from the beginning of time to surround himself with music, of all genres. It was his vice, his talent, his tool. The melody was haunting, and Keket knew she would never forget it. At the end of the main road into the city, there were seven distinct buildings circling the throne room of Abaddon. The horrifyingly realistic statues in the forefront of each structure made identification easy. The figures, all animals, were carved entirely of black lava and littered with precious gemstones.

Standing at the entrance to the House of Pride was a Leviathan, a primordial sea monster, feared for its massive size and strength. A magnificent dragon graced the House of Greed. Its nostrils were flared, and wings extended from its elegant body, as if it was about to take flight. The House of Lust was guarded by another reptile known for its sly nature and stealth attack, the serpent. Green jewels winked at Keket from the eye sockets of the snake. Next in line was the House of Envy with its lone wolf, eyes watching intently, teeth bared. A gargantuan pig and a nondescript ugly goat lounged in front of the House of Gluttony and the House of Sloth, respectively. The House of Wrath was last. A fabulous lion with a thick mane stood defiantly at its door. Keket loved the symbolism of each house's animal.

Occupying the center of Gehenna itself, within the circle of the Houses, was the seat of Abaddon. Keket and her father dismounted and climbed the marble steps of the grand and austere building to meet their Prince. Inside, there was no sound but the clipping of Keket's boots on the marble floor. Extraordinary works of art and sculpture decorated the walls and halls, each depicting the Prince of Darkness himself. Keket wasn't surprised. Her Prince was the most perfectly made of all of Elohim's creations. Scáth guards, armed with wicked swords and shields, lined the long hall. When the great doors opened slowly, they were escorted into the throne room by a massive Scáth on either side.

"Approach," a voice hissed. Standing next to the throne was a wicked looking Scáth clad in a dark robe.

She and her father approached the throne. The seat itself was carved from black marble and sat on a raised dais surrounded by blue flaming water. The entire room was cast in the same ethereal blue as the city. A violent quake of thunder boomed, signaling the arrival of the ruler of Gehenna.

"Abaddon, the Prince of Darkness, the morning star, the seal of perfection, full of wisdom and perfect in beauty. He is the anointed one, ruler of demons, and god of this world. You will bow in our Lord's presence."

She and her father immediately took a knee.

"Rise," the Scáth hissed.

On the dark throne sat the most perfectly beautiful creature ever created by Elohim. Keket could find no words that could describe him. Even though she had been in his presence before, he still took her breath away. She found the longer she looked straight at him, the more nauseous she would feel until her knees would go weak and she would tremble violently. She looked away for a moment to steady herself.

When he spoke, the voice she heard was her own. It did not discombobulate her as it once had. Abaddon was speaking, even though his mouth wasn't moving, but the voice was definitely hers. She knew it would be the same for her father. No wonder the Prince of Darkness found it so easy to manipulate humans. His wishes, his desires, his evil plans were all expressed in that little voice they heard in their heads. Humans had no idea it was the voice of Abaddon himself directing their destruction and journey to darkness. If humans trusted no one and listened to no one, they would never fail to trust or listen to themselves. Who else better understood their needs, knew the desires or wanted to please them than themselves?

"Keket, to me," Abaddon beckoned.

She joined her Prince beside his throne. A sharp jolt of electricity coursed through her veins as she joined her Prince on the dais. She couldn't deny the thrill she experienced knowing she would soon be here beside him for eternity.

"I, too, anticipate our future, my love."

When she realized Abaddon's mouth wasn't moving even though she was hearing these words, she looked sharply at her father.

"Do not be anxious, your father is oblivious," Abaddon soothed. "Our plan? Your brother? All is in motion?"

She bent her head to him acknowledging her yes.

"Your father has overstepped—thinking to conquer me— the splendid one! I will destroy him for his arrogance. I am beyond compare. I will rule this world and the next."

"Oh, splendid one," Keket announced for all to hear. "I am unworthy of this great honor. I live to please you, my prince."

At that, Abaddon smiled slightly and turned his attention to Cain.

"She pleases me, Cain. You do not! To say I am displeased with you Cain would be the understatement of this century," Abaddon spat coldly. "Can you please tell me why you continue to fail so miserably at this simple task I have given you?"

"I have no excuse, my master," Cain countered humbly. "We have been victorious throughout the centuries. It will be no different this time."

"When the last one is reborn, the sign of the one will become the sign of the many. As foretold this promise will usher in the unity of the Light. You know this better than anyone, Cain. You were there when Elohim spoke," Abaddon mused.

"Elohim's plan for the Sorcha will not come to pass. I swear it!" Cain vowed.

"Words, Cain. Simple, empty, disappointing," Abaddon said quietly with no emotion. "I think perhaps you need some incentive, and that is why I called your lovely Keket here to bear witness."

Blue flames shot instantly from Abaddon's eyes and wrapped Cain in a tight coil of pulsing electricity. Keket was sure the pain must have been excruciating.

"Look at your daughter now, you imbecile," Abaddon commanded.

Keket knew the voice her father was hearing was his own, which made it all the more painful.

"She sees you now for what you are, Cain. Weak. Prideful. Ridiculously inept. Look at how she pities you," Abaddon commanded.

Keket schooled her face—wanting her father to see there exactly what her master suggested. When Cain turned his eyes toward her, they were full of an emotion unknown to her—fear. Realization dawned for the first time and she relished it. She understood now that her father was beneath her in all things that mattered: strength, intellect, and emotion. She was better than him, her creator, her father, and always would be. Nothing would stop her now. Her Prince had given her exactly what she needed. She now had the undoubtable confidence within herself that she could and would overthrow her father when the strategy was weaved, the plan complete and the time was right.

"Keket, my love, full of power and worthy beyond all who live in the darkness or the light, you are my greatest treasure," Abaddon praised.

The voice was hers, and as a result, her prince's words meant even more to her. She believed him. She trusted him.

She would fulfill his every command. And in turn, he would make her the queen of all creation.

Abaddon released Cain from his deadly blue embrace. Her father sputtered and then rose to his feet. His head remained bowed showing his deference for his prince, his tormentor.

"Do not fail me again, Cain," Abaddon ordered. "If you do, you will spend your eternity with my human pets in the lake of fire. Do we have an accord?"

"Yes, my prince," Cain answered then extended his hand to her. "Keket? We have much to do."

"We both do," she answered. She bowed to Abaddon and followed her father from the hall, anxious to begin.

CHAPTER 20

Tall Betsy

• • •

JAMIE CROSSED THE YARD AND moved into the shadows of trees that separated the house from the chapel. He pulled his hoodie up to ward off the chill of the October night and hopefully fade into the darkness. He didn't want to be late for his rendezvous with the others. They had decided to wait until after dinner, when most everyone would have settled down for the night. It was late but not too late for what they had planned.

It had all been his idea. He couldn't take the boredom any longer. Even though classes provided a bit of distraction, he missed his freedom. He wanted to laugh, run free. It had been weeks since he and Ioan had arrived at Centenary to start their new wild and crazy life. Since being here, he hadn't seen anything but the classroom, the training room, and Mia's house. He was antsy to explore beyond the boundary. He knew it was forbidden but he had never cared much for rules. Besides, it was Halloween and there was going to be a big party downtown, and Jamie never missed a party.

Growing up on the streets of Dublin had made him tough. He had learned to fight and defend himself. He had learned to take opportunities when they were presented. And if opportunity didn't knock, he had also learned to make it happen for himself. Life was too short for schedules and doing the right thing all the time. He wanted to live a little. The pressures of training along with the reality of the responsibility that lay ahead only made him want to forget about it all for a bit. He knew Ioan would definitely be against it. But what could it hurt? He was smart, he was quick, and best of all he was the Crafter—the coolest gift of them all as far as he was concerned. His ability to create whatever he needed when he needed it had given a tremendous boost to his confidence.

Outside the boundary, Jamie didn't doubt his ability to evade the Scáths and take care of himself. But first he had to find a way out and then back through the supernatural boundary created by the Dìonadain to keep him in and evil out. He also needed to do this without Shen, his katana-carrying warrior angel, finding out. Jamie had considered his options and decided he would have to have help. He needed to find a partner in crime, a street savvy risk-taker anxious for a little change in scenery. It hadn't taken him long to decide just who he needed to persuade.

Jamie had found them earlier that day sitting together on a bench in the park behind the chapel. At one end, Rafe sat, ear buds in, legs kicked out in front of him, lost in his jazz music. Dressed in his customary "smart-guy" nerd t-shirt and leather jacket, Rafe was nothing if not predictable. Today, he wore the face of Albert Einstein. The young man who had grown up on the streets of Atlanta was obsessed with intelligence, his own as well as a few others', as long as their IQ score was ranked at genius level. At the other end, Wei was sitting cross-legged, eating a pop-tart and twirling a fiery orange leaf in her hand that had fallen from the maple tree standing tall above them. Her signature New York Yankee baseball cap was pulled low on her small face.

Both, to Jamie's delight, looked especially bored. He had figured the Knower, gifted with intellect and the ability to solve problems, could figure a way for them to escape undetected by their Dìonadain guardians, while the Wielder could deal with the shield boundary. Besides, he, Rafe and Wei had a lot in common—growing up without parents, in rough neighborhoods, doing what they had to get by. Jamie was betting a few hours in town enjoying live music and Halloween festivities would be an easy sell to them both. It didn't take long for Rafe and Wei to agree to the evening adventure and make a plan for escape. Jamie had found two kindred spirits!

Jamie exited the tree line at the same time as Rafe. They moved quickly to the gate at the crypt where Wei was waiting.

"You're both late," Wei whispered impatiently. "We're gonna miss the band."

"Relax, Yankee, this is gonna be a blast," Jamie grinned.

"Right, exactly what I was thinking!' she answered sarcastically. "Three Light-bearers on the lamb, looking for a good time, dive straight into the mouth of the beast."

"Zip it, Debbie Downer," Rafe ordered. "Are you in or not?"

"Of course, I'm in," Wei said smartly. "Like either one of you could do this without me."

"She's got a point," Jamie laughed. "I can hear the music from here."

"Ok, just like we planned," Rafe said. "Wei, is the lookout. J comes with me and watches my back while I find a way to disarm whatever device is tracking us within the shield."

"Be quick," Wei said. "I can literally smell the caramel apples and kettle corn from here."

"Let's go," Rafe said unlatching the gate to the crypt.

Jamie followed him in. They left Wei behind to act as lookout.

Jamie had been in his fair share of weird places but this was by far the creepiest.

"No wonder this is an entrance to the Hall below. Who would want to ever hang out in here long enough to find anything?"

"Yeah, it's perfectly terrifying," Rafe agreed, pushing a stone jar in one of the vaults back into a recess, tripping the opening to the floor below.

"Welcome to the super top secret, have to kill you if you know about it, entrance to the Hall of the Sorcha," Rafe announced with a grin.

Jamie followed him down the circular stone steps into the labyrinth of tunnels, halls and rooms under the grounds of Centenary College. This was definitely not boring! A thrill of excitement swam around in his gut. Just like he had planned, they hadn't seen or heard a Dìonadain guard yet. The warrior angels were at prayer in the sanctuary above. Within the perimeter, the Sorcha could come and go as they pleased. They were allowed this freedom because of the impenetrable shield surrounding the campus grounds. They also tracked the whereabouts of the Light-bearers constantly with the use of the globe in the Dìonadain Council room.

In no time, they entered through a natural rock archway across a stone threshold into the Council room. It was empty. In the center of the room was a large stone table and four seats, Jamie knew must be for the Council members. Suspended above the table was an iridescent globe marking the exact movements of the Light-bearers. Jamie counted eleven stars on the globe all bunched together in the same grid. Under the globe, built into the center of the table was a device that looked like a codex, with its cogs and symbols.

"This looks complicated," Jamie mused thoughtfully. "Not sure how you are gonna pull this off."

"Not your job to worry about it, bro," Rafe boasted. "I got this. Now, watch the entrance."

Jamie watched Rafe move the dials of the codex back and forth working them into a sequence only the Knower would understand. Jamie smirked, thinking the codex was like an ancient Rubik's cube.

"The door? If you don't mind," Rafe said smartly.

Jamie turned his back on Rafe and kept watch. He didn't want to be surprised by a Dìonadain who had finished his prayers early.

"None the wiser. We are good to go, my man," Rafe said walking toward the door.

"Are you sure? That was awful quick," Jamie remarked.

"You have no idea who you are dealing with," Rafe said smugly. "Come on."

Jamie followed Rafe out of the chamber and back up to the crypt where Wei was waiting impatiently.

"I could have eaten three caramel apples by now," she said sarcastically.

"How is it that one so small can eat as much as you do?" Jamie asked.

"She may be little but she packs a big punch!" Rafe interjected. "Wei eats more than me and Lucas put together most of the time."

"Boys, do you want to stand around and talk about my eating habits or do you want to go to the party?"

"By all means, my lady, lead on," Jamie challenged with a wink and a grin.

"Follow me, gentleman, and be truly amazed," Wei said moving quickly to the edge of the Centenary property.

Jamie could hear the low-keyed hum of the protective shield.

"You haven't seen my girl in action yet," Rafe said to Jamie. "Wei's gift will blow your mind."

"Ok, Yankee, show me what you can do," Jamie challenged good-naturedly.

Wei turned her cap around backwards and faced the invisible shield. She extended both arms, palms out, and pushed them forward into the shield. Light sparked and hissed around her hands. Jamie watched as she closed her eyes and pushed harder against the barrier. The light grew, and when Wei spread her hands wider, an opening in the shield appeared. She opened it large enough for them to pass through. Rafe went through first and then Jamie followed him. When Wei stepped through the light disappeared and the shield closed behind her.

Wei reached into the pockets of her leather jacket and pulled out three plain black masks.

"Seriously, a Batman mask?" Rafe asked.

"And feathers? You want me to wear feathers?" Jamie asked.

"We need to fit in," she explained. "It is Halloween after all. I didn't have much choice when I raided Audrey's Halloween storage boxes."

Jamie donned his mask and grinned, "Let's go trick or treat!"

The trio laughed. They walked quickly down the street toward the sound of music and the crowd of people gathered downtown for the Halloween festival. Caught up in the thrill of the adventure, Jamie didn't notice the dark figures slipping out of the trees along the sidewalk and from around the corners of the dark alleys they passed.

Rounding the corner, Jamie was bombarded by the sights, sounds and smells of Halloween. People were milling about everywhere, young and old, dressed as their favorite scary or cartoon character. Food trucks lined the street. Bright lights hung from the trees and buildings. In the center of the town square, a large stage was set up for the country-rock band performing.

"Hey, first one to find Tall Betsy gets a mug of cider, my treat," Jamie offered.

Tall Betsy was the official Halloween goblin of the town. Local legend told of a tall woman dressed in black that would steal little children who lurked outside after dark on Halloween. Every year, Tall Betsy would make an appearance at the party, roaming among the people, much to their fright and delight. Jamie scanned the crowd looking for the spooky goblin. Instead, he found a Pink Lady and two T-Birds.

"Well, if it isn't tall, dark and dreamy?" the pink lady with the honey-sweet voice flirted with Rafe. "Introductions?"

"Yes, please," Jamie urged with a mischievous grin.

"Reese Pooley, Gray Lee and Marshall Cooper, these are my friends, Jamie Taryn and Wei Sung."

"Y'all been laying low, man?" Gray commented. "Outside of chemistry class, I haven't seen you or Lucas in ages."

"Aww, you miss me?" Rafe asked laughing. "I'm moved, man, really I am."

Gray continued, "What about Aiden? He's all but disappeared since school started. Do you know what's going on with him?"

Reese offered with great disdain, "I'm guessing our sweet little Lily has been keeping him company?"

"Nah, I think Lily kicked the habit. I haven't seen Aiden and I don't want to," Rafe commented derisively.

"Why so touchy?" Marshall asked. "I thought Aiden and the Quinns were one big happy family?"

"Well, you thought wrong," Rafe said with thinly veiled anger.

"Hey, it was nice meeting all of you, but, we have to be somewhere, right guys?" Wei hurried moving in the opposite direction.

"Yeah, right, great seeing y'all," Rafe responded following her. "Let's go, Jamie."

"Watch out for Tall Betsy," Marshall shouted before disappearing in the crowd with his friends.

Jamie turned on Wei. "Hey, what's your problem? They seemed friendly enough."

"Not from what I've heard. I'll fill you in later," she answered.

"Let's go hear the band," Rafe suggested.

"I think we should stick together," Wei shouted above the din of the band.

"Agreed," Rafe said. "We don't want to take too many chances."

"Sure thing," Jamie added. "But seriously, I think this place is harmless and if something did happen, we could handle it, right?"

Wei and Rafe looked at each other and then back at him. "Of course," they answered in unison.

After listening to music, eating a ridiculous amount of candy and playing corn hole, Jamie suggested, "We better head back. The crowd is starting to thin out."

"Yeah, blending in is gonna be more difficult the longer we stay," Wei added.

"I know a shortcut back to Centenary, come on," Rafe urged.

Jamie followed Rafe and Wei. The farther they got from the crowd the more unsettled he felt. It was dark. They were alone. They were targets after all. It would be easy for the Scáths to overpower and outnumber them. Now that the thrill of sneaking outside of Centenary had worn off, he was beginning to question the wisdom of their plan. He shook it off and chalked it up to a spooky Halloween night.

"Hey, J, better late than never, but I think I just found Tall Betsy," Rafe boasted.

Turning the corner into a dimly lit alley, Jamie came up behind Rafe and Wei. Sure enough, there she was. Eight-foot tall, dark and supremely ugly—it was Tall Betsy—or at least whoever was getting paid that night to dress up and entertain the crowds. She walked slowly down the alleyway. Jamie, Rafe and Wei continued in her direction but stopped when two more Tall Betsys appeared behind the first.

"This alley just got real crowded," Jamie warned softly.

"Let's turn back," Rafe agreed.

Turning around, they were greeted by another group of Tall Betsy figures—only this group was hissing.

"I'm thinking we're gonna get a chance to see what we're made of, boys," Wei mused, moving in front of Jamie and Rafe.

"Got any ideas?" Jamie said quickly to Rafe.

"Yeah, I'm thinking we're idiots and we should've stayed behind that shield," Rafe quipped.

"My bad, bro, I'm sorry," Jamie offered.

"Will you two shut up and think about us getting out of here alive?" Wei shouted.

"Way ahead of you, Yankee," Jamie said. He had reached down and picked up some glass from the street.

"Here," Jamie handed Rafe a short sword fashioned from the glass, "Use this when they get close."

When the dark figures' eyes blazed blue, Jamie's worst suspicions were confirmed. He shouted, "Here we go!"

The trio stood back to back ready to fight the demon Scáths closing in.

Lightning struck the street below them surrounding them in flashes of white hot light. The ground rumbled below Jamie's feet, when Shen, Agatha, and Kiefer landed solidly in front of them, encircling them in a golden pulsing light. Blue and golden flames clashed in a rainbow of light. Jamie's last coherent thought was the discomfort he felt when Shen grabbed him in the iron grip of wings and rocketed up into the dark sky.

● ● ●

She was disappointed.

She had left her home far behind—a stranger in an even stranger land.

Nonetheless, she had embraced her task with a spirit of hope.

Surely, the journey wasn't for naught?

Did they even have the ability required to complete the task?

Foolish and immature,

Only thinking about themselves,

Would they be steadfast in the face of challenge, pain, and perhaps even death?

They had used their gifts for selfish gain and not for Elohim's purpose.

Their folly had almost killed them.

She grasped her chest and breathed sharply.

She felt small shards of cold ice burrowing into her heart.

It was an emotion unknown to her until now.

It was fear.

If the Light-bearers continued to look within, focusing on their own desires, they would surely fail.

She was sure of this truth now more than ever before.

The power of the darkness was growing.

She lifted her gaze to the night sky and found the brightest star.

She breathed deeply focusing on the pinpoint of pure light.

It calmed her.

The star reminded her of home, her family, her mission, and most importantly, her Creator.

Her heart warmed as it settled on the truth resonating there.
I will not fear for Elohim is with me.
I will not lose hope because I know Elohim will strengthen me and help me.
She was a Natsar.
She would do what she must.
She would watch over them and their future.

CHAPTER 21

Roar

• • •

"Seriously, Rafe, how could you be so stupid?!" Lucas shouted.

"I know man. I got no excuse," Rafe hung his head.

"Not only did you and Jamie put us all at risk, you could have ruined any chance at all of us winning this fight."

"It wasn't his idea, Luc," Jamie said. "I take full responsibility."

"Whatever, you both were only thinking of yourselves. It was all just about a good time. Am I right? Have you forgotten what we are all part of?"

"Luc, yes, it was selfish, we are idiots, but we never meant to put anyone at risk," Wei said softly.

"I can't even talk to you right now, Wei," Lucas said. "Of all people, I thought you would get it."

"I do, Lucas," Wei pleaded. "The pressure of it all got to me. I'm so sorry."

Lucas rolled his eyes. Then he stared down all three of his friends. "Don't ever scare me like that again, you got it?"

"Absolutely," they chimed in.

"We learned our lesson, I promise," Wei responded and nodded her head toward Agatha, who was standing a short distance away, her face rigid as stone. "And I don't mean what happened in that alley. Have you ever seen an angry Dìonadain? I don't recommend it."

Lucas grinned. "I'll remember that."

He walked away from his three contrite friends and into the training area. Sequestered in the Hall of the Sorcha, deep under the grounds of Centenary College, Lucas and the other Light-bearers trained. With the help of their Dìonadain guardians, they pushed themselves to explore the Light within them. They practiced their skills developing precision, control and focus. Lucas knew they were close, only one more Light-bearer to discover. The uniting would happen. He no longer doubted but anticipated it. Once they found the book they would win this war, and Aiden would finally pay for what he had done. Lucas hadn't given up his anger toward Aiden; it had only intensified. He worked hard to hide it from the others, knowing they would tell him to let it go and focus on the task before them. But he wanted Aiden to pay for what he had done. He wanted all of them to pay—for Aunt Scarlet's death, his mother's kidnapping, Lily's broken heart, his own pain at Aiden's betrayal. But most of all he wanted justice for his father's death. A reckoning was coming for the Talbot family, and Lucas would lead the charge.

"Put your back into it!" Lucas urged.

"I'd like to see you do any better, Captain America," Ioan shouted back good-naturedly tossing a slab of granite like it was a piece of bread.

Ioan had tagged him with the nickname right after they had met. It had stuck, and he wasn't gonna lie, he kinda liked it. The Warrior was truly a sight to behold, all muscle and grit. Every day, with each training session, Ioan advanced. It wouldn't be long before the Irishman would be lifting semi-trucks and knocking down stone walls with his bare hands.

"Focus, Warrior," Makaio thundered, coming up behind Ioan and placing him swiftly in a chokehold.

Lucas laughed good-naturedly when Ioan sputtered, struggling to break the hold of the mighty Dìonadain. A savage roar sounded from the largest training room, jarring him from his thoughts. Lucas turned to watch the action inside. Inside the room, Ioan, Lily and Harper were being challenged by their guardians, Makaio, Jude and Cora. The tremendous sound, Lucas likened to a jungle animal, had come from Harper, the Psalter. Lucas had marveled when he had been told of Harper's voice breaking chains and tumbling walls. But what she was doing now was wicked cool!

With the help of her guardian, Cora, Harper was learning to focus her voice. When Harper roared, the large pieces of granite Ioan was holding would explode and crumble to dust. Challenging the Warrior's strength and focusing the Psalter's voice, the Dìonadain pushed Ioan and Harper mercilessly. Both Light-bearers were dripping with perspiration. It wasn't in either of their natures to quit or ask for a break, so they continued to push back on each other, iron sharpening iron. The rest of the Sorcha gathered round Lucas to watch the action as well.

"I've never seen anything like this," Zoe said in awe. "They're incredible."

"I knew my brother was strong, but this girl is giving him a run for his money," Jamie joked.

"You sound surprised, Jamie," Celeste said. "You would do well to never underestimate the strength or tenacity of a woman."

"At least when you're around, Celeste," Rafe warned. "Am I right, Daniel?"

"Certainly, or any of the other fairest members of our tribe, we are blessed to have them fighting at our sides, gentlemen. We are stronger for it," Daniel smiled.

"Ok, ok, point taken," Jamie laughed. "I know when I've been bested."

"What's with the shades?" Lucas nudged Daniel who was standing beside him.

Daniel took off his sunglasses revealing his tired dark-circled bloodshot eyes.

"You look terrible, man," Lucas said to his friend. "Not sleeping?"

"Not much," Daniel said wryly. "I haven't slept much lately—too much to pray about it seems."

Lucas put his hand on Daniel's shoulder and squeezed it. He knew the burden Daniel carried for them all was a great one. Lucas had often wondered if Daniel wasn't the most important member of their group.

"Hush, something is happening," Wei spoke sharply.

Lucas turned his attention to Lily in the training area. Her eyes were closed and she was very still. Jude, standing behind her, unfurled his wings and wrapped them around her. He lifted her high above the activity below and set her on a stone parapet hanging over the chamber. When Harper opened her mouth again to release the power of the Light within her, his sister opened her eyes and shouted, "Cease!"

Lucas had never heard the tone or measure of authority that was in his sister's voice before. When Lily spoke again, Lucas knew they were hearing a prophetic word from the Dreamer.

"Thus, saith Elohim, the Creator of all things in heaven and earth. I afflicted Ariel, and I heard her great sadness and weeping. But she is to me like a lion. I settled against her all around. I besieged her with towers. I raised strongholds against her."

At Lily's words, towers of stone emerged from the ground below Harper and Ioan. The ground shook violently as the towers were literally built from the sand of the training room floor. Lucas couldn't believe what he was witnessing. But it was real. Makaio and Cora soared above the chamber leaving Ioan and Harper alone below. Ioan leapt toward Harper to protect her. But, he was pulled back down by two arms of swirling sand. Ioan struggled but was buried up to his shoulders within the sand. He couldn't move or break free.

Harper was left alone to battle the swirling sand. Slews of arrows were released from the tower battlements. Harper roared stopping them cold. But the arrows started coming faster. One found its mark. Harper fell to the ground a golden arrow buried deep in her chest.

Lily continued, "She was brought low; from the earth she spoke, and from the dust her speech blessed me; her voice came from the ground like the voice of a ghost, a whisper."

Lucas stood and shouted, "No!"

Daniel grabbed his arm and pulled him back down, "It's not over, watch."

Harper was spent, the blood pouring from her wound soaked her shirt. Her face, now pale and drawn, looked like a ghost. Ioan yelled in anguish unable to protect her. Harper was oblivious to it all. She began to sing softly. Lily continued her prophecy.

"Now the multitude of her enemies are like dust beneath her feet and the multitude of the ruthless like grains of sand blowing in the wind. Without warning, I visited her, with thunder and with earthquake and great noise, with whirlwind and tempest, and the flame of a devouring fire."

A loud clap of thunder filled the room and a rush of wind followed. Lucas watched as a whirlwind suspended Harper in the middle of the chamber while a flame ignited, wild and raging, it toppling the towers to dust. The flames were extinguished as quickly as they had come. The whirlwind dropped Harper and then sucked up all the sand, releasing its hold on Ioan, and then it disappeared with a loud boom. Harper stood, without blemish or injury, and faced Lily. Her whole countenance was changed—a dauntless courage shone brightly on her face.

"Now, the multitude of all the dark ones that fight against Ariel, all that fight against her and her stronghold and distress her, shall be like a dream, a vision of the night."

Lily bowed her head and sunk to ground weeping. Harper sunk to her knees. Her body convulsing with a deep welling of emotion and experience that Lucas could only wonder at. When Cora, Harper's guardian, glowed hot molten gold and extended her massive wings sending a rush of mighty wind throughout the training chamber, Harper stood.

Cora drew her flaming broadsword and spoke, "You will from this day forth be called Ariel, the Lioness of El, victorious under Elohim. Your voice will be like a lion—a roar that will topple strongholds, turning your enemies to dust. Like a hurricane that bends and breaks things in its path, you will lead the charge of the Sorcha. You, Ariel, Psalter and Light-bearer, are highly favored by Elohim."

Harper turned and spoke to everyone in the chamber, "Light-bearers, though we are flesh and blood, we do not battle according to our physical form, for the weapons of our warfare are not of the flesh, but divine, powerful and unyielding, gifts from Elohim used by us to destroy fortresses of darkness."

A hush spread over the room, every Light-bearer recognizing the burden of their gift. Lucas was overwhelmed with the sense of purpose he felt not only for himself but for these people around him—once strangers but now family.

"Everyone, please," Daniel urged. "I have something I need to say."

Ten young men and women gathered around Daniel. Lucas sensed the significance of what Daniel was going to share. The atmosphere in the room felt heavy. It was the same feeling he had when he first set foot in the Citadel. This room was sacred space right now.

Daniel began, "Ariel has spoken truth today. Our struggle is not against flesh and blood, but against the rulers, powers, and forces of darkness and wickedness surrounding us. We must all commit to something right here and right now if we have any shot at all of winning our fight."

"I think we're ready to do whatever we must Daniel. We've all shown that. What more could we do?" Celeste asked.

Daniel nodded and continued, "Our victory will not come from our own strength or intellect, Celeste. We will not triumph of our own accord by using our own gifts, as incredible as they are. It all means nothing!"

"Then, how?" Jamie asked. "How will we win?"

"We will only vanquish the enemy through the power of the spirit of Elohim that lives within us. Only by Him are all things done. It's the only way we win this thing before us. That means it's on us to make sure there is no emotion, action or thought in our mind or spirit that will stand in the way. When we find number twelve, when we unite, it can only be the Light living in us, bold, pure and good," Daniel finished.

"Daniel is right," Lucas agreed. He met the eyes of every Light-bearer and continued, "I am so proud of all of us. We've worked so hard to get to this place. I know you all feel it just like I do. We are close. We can't lose faith. We need to do as Daniel says and search our hearts. We have to be ready."

Wei urged quietly. "Daniel, we need you to pray for us."

The Sorcha circled up and linked hands. Daniel led them in a prayer for guidance, humility, favor and provision. When Daniel was finished, Lucas felt a definite shift in the air. It was practically humming with power of the Light.

"What happens now, Luc?" Lily asked pulling him to the side.

"What do you mean?" Lucas probed.

Lily continued, "My dreams are getting sharper. It seriously could happen at any moment—number twelve, I mean. I can't see who it is, but I know they are coming toward us. Is it wrong that I'm a little afraid?"

Lucas squeezed her hand, "Nah, it will keep you sharp. At least it does me."

"We can't do anything without our Leader. I think it must be someone older? Don't you?"

"I just hope whoever he or she is will be prepared to lead us courageously. Leadership is about respect," Lucas said seriously.

Their conversation was interrupted when Nolan announced, "Light-bearers, please take your place in the Hall of the Sorcha. It's time for a history lesson."

Still reeling from what they had just witnessed, as well as carrying the weight of the burden before them, Lucas and the others left the training chamber. A bright light, shining from a large silver orb suspended from the ceiling, illuminated the chamber. Huge stone columns covered in ancient script surrounded the long rectangular space. Between each column stood a life-size marble statue. At the foot of each statue was a seat carved into the base of the statue itself. Eleven Light-bearers took their place. Nolan, his wings folded behind him, stood quietly in the middle of the space. Asher joined him. The remaining Dìonadain guard stood round their Light-bearers.

Nolan began, "Soon, the last member of your group will emerge. When your number is twelve and the circle is complete, you will be able to unite the Light that lives in each of you. Then and only then will you possess the power to find Simon's book."

"But none of that will matter if you don't have the key that unlocks the secret of Simon's book—the key he gave his son Ahmlaid on the night that he was murdered," Asher continued.

"How are we going to find Ahmlaid? How do we know where the key is?"

"I might be able to point you in the right direction," Asher said.

A swirling mist filled the space. Within the thick vapor, images took shape. Asher was creating a vision they could all see. Lucas and the others had seen this stone circle with its executioner's slab in the center before. It was the site of Simon's murder. But this time, Lucas knew they were seeing the events from an entirely different perspective, Asher's point of view. Lucas sat forward slightly anticipating the real-life story about to unfold.

CHAPTER 22

Truth

• • •

THE FRENZIED MOB SPIT CURSES and screamed for the death of the Light-bearer. Simon was bound, his arms and legs stretched so tightly, his joints were dislocated. He must have been in excruciating pain, but Simon's face, smeared with blood and mud, was emotionless. Asher knew Simon understood his time on this earth was finished, his task was complete. Elohim would welcome him home before the hour passed.

Asher caught Nolan's bleak eye from across the angry crowd. Asher shared Nolan's somber feelings. They would lose another Light-bearer tonight, for they had been betrayed by their brother. The next twenty-four hours would be the most critical of their assignment. There was much to lose if they failed. Yet if they succeeded with the plan, the world and the future of the Sorcha would be secure. Asher knew timing would be tricky, but luckily their presence had not yet been detected. The only one who would have recognized them in their rough wool cloaks and hoods was Cain. But the traitor, their brother in arms, was too busy playing to the crowd.

Nolan's mission was Ahmlaid. He was to guard Simon's son and aid him in his escape. Ahmlaid carried the key to his father's book, the key that would unlock the power of its words. Asher's path lay in a different direction altogether. He steeled himself, ready to make his move, his eyes never leaving Cain.

"Kill him, kill him," the crowd chanted loudly.

Asher watched Cain raise a wicked steel saw in his hand. The long thick blade was edged with jagged teeth. It would be a gruesome death. The Light-bearer's lips were moving. Asher knew without doubt that Elohim heard Simon's whispered words.

Because he was standing so close to the executioner's slab, Asher could hear them as well.

"Though I walk through the valley of the shadow of death I will not fear. You comfort me Elohim. Into your hands, I give my body, soul and spirit."

"Amen," Asher whispered, "and well-done my friend."

The crowd quieted when Cain laid the saw across Simon's exposed midsection.

"Darkness has been waiting for you, Light-bearer."

Asher marked the cold blue flame that ignited in Cain's eyes, right before his first pull on the saw. The blade cut raggedly into Simon's gut. A blinding light burst forth from the wound. The people fell back. Asher knew the once-confident mob would now be frightened. He was sure none had ever witnessed a light so bright or a death so bizarre. Ignoring the distressed crowd, Asher kept his eyes on the executioner. Cain was studying the etchings on the blade that had been made by the blinding light.

When the crowd started to panic, Cain rested the saw against the slab and turned to calm the fray. Asher moved quickly. One moment could make all the difference. He reached for the saw and hid it under his cloak so quickly it went without notice. He faded silently into the confusion of the crowd, disappearing into the darkness of the surrounding forest. When he was sure no one had followed him, Asher threw off his cloak and shot into the sky, the saw tucked under his arm. For anyone below who happened to look up, his trajectory looked like a white-hot shooting star and would be taken as a good omen.

Asher landed silently on the shore of a rocky island. The sound of the waves gently rolling in to the shore was peaceful. It was desolate here, quiet and lonely. The perfect place to hide, a forgotten land.

"He is gone?" an old man asked quietly from the shadows.

"It was a good death," Asher replied. "No pain—only peace and victory."

"The key is safe?"

"Simon's boy escaped with it. Nolan will keep him safe until he can secure the key at the appointed place."

"Ahmlaid is a good man. He will do what his father asked, maybe too well. Simon chose well. He will make the task difficult for the next twelve.

"As it should be," Asher responded. "We surely cannot help them find it. It will be up to them. And we can take no chances."

"Never underestimate the evil that seeks the Light, Asher."

The two stood companionably in silence for a while. Each reflecting on the incredible events that had led them to this moment.

"Do you mourn your lost brother?" the old man asked.

"No," Asher replied strongly. "Cain has made his choice. He has already destroyed himself. He just doesn't know it yet. He is a selfish, greedy coward."

"Is this the blade that took Simon's life?"

"Yes, when Cain cut Simon, the power of the Light within him burst forth and burned these markings into the blade."

The old man reached for the saw. He ran his fingers across the etchings.

"Brilliant," he whispered in awe. "Simon was nothing if not thorough. He left nothing to chance if he could help it."

"What do you mean?"

"It's a map!" the old man smiled gently. "The Light marked the saw with these symbols that will guide the twelve once they unite to the location of Ahmlaid and the key."

"Undeniably brilliant," Asher agreed. "We must keep it safe until it is needed by the twelve."

"The protection of the saw will not be my task to fulfill. I am weary, Asher. My time is near."

"Don't say that, John," Asher urged. "We still have much to do."

"My book is almost finished. The dreams have taken their toll on me of late. When the revelations stop coming, I will be finished here on this earth."

"You need to rest, John," Asher urged gently. "I will watch over you while you sleep."

"You have always been there for me, my friend," John buried his hand in Asher's wing and laid his head on his guardian's shoulder as he had done since their first meeting so long ago. "I must ask for your help one last time."

"And I will provide it," Asher said solemnly. He knew John was speaking the truth. He would not be here much longer.

"Elohim has shown me the path of the saw. When I am gone, I want you to take it across the sea to an island of green. It is an ancient place of dark magic and idol worship. Give it to the Celtic chieftain named Ó'Cuinn. He is a good and wise king. He will follow the Light after he meets you. Teach him. Train him. He and his descendants will protect the saw for many generations to come. It is important that the saw remain in his family line."

"It's too risky, John," Asher countered. "The saw must stay with the Dionadain. We are the only ones who can protect it. Cain won't stop looking for it. I believe he considers it a trophy of Simon's death. If it were to fall into his hands, the map to the key might be lost forever."

"The light still shines in the darkness and the darkness will not conquer it. You will do as I ask, Asher," John commanded gently. "You have not seen the future, but I have. The O'Cuinn will keep it safe—hidden from the world until it is time."

"It will be so, John," Asher vowed.

"Tell them something for me, will you? The twelve to come?"

"Of course," Asher answered.

"They must be sober-minded, vigilant at all times. Abaddon is the fiercest enemy they will ever know. He is hungry for them, to devour the Light within them. It gives him power. They must withstand him, be immovable in their faith when they are tested. For they will be, all of them."

The mist dissipated and along with it the images of Asher and John. Whispers and murmurs filled the space. The Lightbearers were amazed by what they had just seen and by what they now knew about the saw.

Rafe spoke above the din. "Excellent! All we have to do is find the descendants of the O'Cuinn and we find the saw. I'll start researching it now."

"You don't have to, Rafe," Lucas said quietly. "They're sitting in this room right now."

"O'Cuinn is an ancient surname of Ireland. Today, the name is Quinn," Beni said.

"This day just keeps getting better!" Rafe responded. "Why keep it a secret, man? You have the saw."

"Not anymore," Lucas said regretfully. "When I was a kid my dad showed it to me. It was super cool, very old and covered with symbols. It was just hanging on a wall in his woodshop. No big deal. He told me it was a family heirloom and would be mine one day to pass on to my son."

"Just like John said to Asher," Beni said. "For thousands of years the Quinn family has protected the saw."

"Until me," Lucas said with anger. "The day my dad was murdered, we ran. I forgot about the saw. I left it there."

"Don't beat yourself up, Luc. You were just a kid; how could you have known?" Wei reassured.

Lucas squeezed Wei's hand acknowledging her support. "Thanks, Wei. But, it doesn't change the fact that I failed."

"Ok, so let's go back, the saw might still be there, right?" Zoe asked. "Our house was in the middle of nowhere in the mountains. Everything might be just as we left it. It's worth a shot!"

"It's not there," Lucas said quietly.

"How do you know, man? We have to try," Rafe returned.

"I know because I've seen it recently. I didn't recognize it at the time but it was the saw. Man, how could I have been such an idiot?!" Lucas exclaimed.

"I got a really bad feeling we aren't going to like what you say next, bro," Rafe said.

"Where is the saw, Luc?" Wei asked.

Lucas looked around the circle. He met the eyes of every Light-bearer, his friends, before he spoke with conviction. "The last place we want to go."

"Tell us, Lucas," Lily urged.

"The saw is hanging above the fireplace in the library of the Talbot mansion."

CHAPTER 23

Challenges

• • •

NOLAN JOINED THE OTHER THREE members of the Dìonadain council around the stone table. Othiel, Chief of the Watchers, little emotion evident in either his face or frame, sat quietly awaiting Nolan to begin. Beside him was Hila, Chief of the Messengers. As usual, Hila was tense, ready to get on with things, so she could return to managing her extensive network of information gathering and delivery. And then there was Andreas, Chief of the Warriors, his comrade in arms, beaming with anticipation and passion. As the leader of the council, Nolan was to give an update on the progress of the Light-bearers. It was a critical time —so much to lose if they failed— so much to gain if the Sorcha united. Strategy and timing were of the essence.

"Let us begin, my brothers and sister. I will give an account of the Light-bearers we have most recently discovered and then we will discuss the others."

"As you wish, Nolan," Othiel responded.

"Celeste Bouchard, the Exiler, is strong in her gift. Surprising, because she has lived in the darkness and its wretched lies for so long. Yet she struggles with thoughts of guilt and shame regarding the family she left behind. They continue to live in the darkness Celeste fled. She is torn between wanting to go back and save them and staying here to complete the task."

"She will have to conquer the guilt that plagues her mind to truly operate in her gift," Hila said.

"Yes. But you and I both know, Hila, guilt is not an enemy to be conquered. It is a perspective to be surrendered. Celeste will never be able eliminate the tension she is experiencing until she resolves within her own heart the regret she has about leaving her family behind."

"Agreed. Celeste must focus on what she has been chosen to do and her mission here. It is the only way she can destroy the darkness consuming her family there," Hila added.

"Moving on, the Taryn brothers are a marvelous and frustrating duo all at the same time," Nolan continued.

"Tell us of Jamie, first," Othiel encouraged.

"Jamie Taryn, the Crafter, is self-assured and a risk-taker," Nolan started.

"What is wrong with that?" boomed Andreas.

"Nothing if he tempers it with some humility, which he does not, yet. His boasting and lack of taking responsibility will continue to get him into trouble, if not. Arrogance is the enemy of humility. Cain will smell it and seek to lure Jamie over to darkness. Only when his gifts are governed by meekness will they reflect the Light."

"We must watch him closely, then," Andreas suggested. "If Jamie only considers his gift something that will bring him fame, he is dangerous and susceptible to weakness."

"His brother, Ioan, the Warrior, has an altogether different challenge. He knows he is stronger than most men. He recognizes his brute strength, yet he still doesn't understand his potential. Within him lies the strength of a hurricane, an earthquake, and a hundred lions," Nolan recounted.

Hila suggested, "But he fears his strength, does he not? Deep down Ioan wrestles with his ability. He fears becoming his father or losing his tender heart in the pursuit of developing his strength."

"Our gentle giant possesses the strength to move mountains when Elohim is guiding him," Othiel continued. "He will come to realize the goodness of his strength. It will just take some time."

"Yes, Othiel, it is as you say. We need him to discover his real strength lies in the goodness of his heart and not in the goodness of his might. Ioan's father never understood this principle. Shifting the Warrior's focus will unlock his discovery of one simple truth, all light derives its strength from love," Nolan articulated.

"Hear, hear!" Andreas agreed. "Tell us of the Psalter."

"Today, something truly miraculous happened in training. Through a prophetic word spoken by Lily, Elohim transformed the identity of Harper Grierson. She is now Ariel, the lioness. This mantle she will now wear will be a challenge to her mind, heart and soul. Ariel must learn to harness the power of her gift, focus it, and remain calm and in control. However, I sense an insecurity in her now, a fear that she will be overwhelmed by her gift and lose herself altogether."

Andreas suggested, "Then she must be taught to understand her transformation incorporates who she was, it does not destroy it. Her transformation furthers her ability and power in the Light."

"True, brother, but I believe the fear Nolan describes may be eclipsed by a greater danger," Othiel predicted.

"Explain," Nolan interjected.

"The Psalter may come to love her gift more than the gift-giver and the Light that has transformed her. To be sure, many will be captivated by the beauty her gift brings. This admiration and attention has the potential to bring great temptation to her," Othiel predicted.

"Othiel is right," Nolan urged. "We must do everything within our power to help Ariel withstand this potential threat. She must remain grounded and pursue an attitude of meekness."

"And the others? How are the first five progressing?" Hila asked pointedly.

"I see signs that Rafe, the Knower, is beginning to struggle with pride. As a strength can, his power may also become his weakness. His gift will be his downfall if not submitted totally to Elohim. Rafe truly believes he is never wrong. He doesn't like to accept direction or views from others. This will be a problem when the Leader emerges and is discovered."

"Keep an eye on him Nolan," Andreas suggested. "I worry about that one."

Othiel and Hila agreed with Andreas' need for caution.

Nolan continued, "Beni is right where he should be in the development of his gift. But, he struggles to find his place in the group. He realizes the amazing power of his gift but does not believe it compares to the gifts of the others. He knows he is needed but wonders if he has value."

Othiel offered, "Not surprising. We all knew it was but a matter of time before the comparisons of one another's gifts would occur. I am just concerned that it has happened to Beni, and he has judged himself to be lacking."

"I share your misgivings, Othiel. If the Speaker continues down this path, he will become bitter and resentful. His insecurity will cause him to doubt his gift. He will be overcome with it. His insecurities will erect barriers between himself and Elohim, prohibiting the true expression of the Light within him."

"Zoe is a friend to him. I will encourage her to support him, help him see his value to the group," Nolan offered.

"And Wei? Her gift is quite powerful and its control even more daunting," Othiel stated.

"She is growing stronger in her gift. Wei does not fear or doubt the power of the Light within her. However, she struggles in another way. She is a loner, afraid to depend on any of the others," Nolan explained.

"She will need to learn the value of vulnerability and trust," Hila urged. "Her gift and its tremendous power come only as a result of her relationship with the Light. As such, her connection with the other Light-bearers is critical. The encouragement of the twelve and their belief in her ability will allow Wei to draw more power from the Light, allowing further growth of her gift. She needs relationship, friendship if you will, with the twelve if she is to survive what it to come."

"And Daniel? Is he struggling?" Othiel asked.

"I am very concerned about young Daniel," Nolan said gravely.

"Why the heavy heart for the Believer, Nolan?" Andreas asked.

"Daniel bears a great burden for the twelve. He shoulders a heavy responsibility for them all. It weighs on him."

"The task is difficult to be sure, but, he must not tire or falter," Hila offered.

"And he realizes that. Daniel is constantly at prayer now, petitioning and interceding on the Sorcha's behalf with Elohim. This reality may eventually create distance between him and the others. Should he withdraw from them, albeit for the noble endeavor of prayer, he risks losing the compassion fueling his faith," Nolan explained.

Andreas added, "He knows who he is praying for, the enormity of the task facing them, and the urgency of their success. He understands how to pray. He needs to stay close to them."

Nolan urged, "I agree with you, my brother. We must be watchful. Prayer gives Daniel a different perspective than the rest but his isolation is not healthy for him as we move forward."

"And the Quinn siblings? Much depends on them. It always has," Othiel interjected.

"Zoe is steady and content, unusual for someone her age. She grows in humility and grace. The Healer's desire is and will continue to be, I think, one for peace, unity, and the continued welfare of the group."

"Wonderful news, Nolan," Othiel said. "Zoe's simple confidence will become the benchmark of unwavering stability the twelve will need to push through the obstacles ahead for them all."

"Othiel is correct in his interpretation," Hila declared. "And Lily? Is she growing in her gift?"

"The Dreamer is actually operating in her gift the most at this juncture in time. Lily dreams almost daily and is able to give prophetic words now. She is bound to sleep now for her dreams, but soon she will have waking visions," Nolan responded.

"And Lucas?" Andreas pushed.

"I am grieved for Lucas. His gift has continued to mature but I believe the Perceiver's true power is now stifled by his anger and resentment toward Aiden Talbot. It is like a cancer, consuming his thoughts, motivating his feelings and behaviors."

"He must not be allowed to continue down this path, Nolan," Andreas said. "Anger is a seed for darkness. Once planted, it will take root. It may destroy everything."

"I know, brother, that's what I am afraid of," Nolan agreed quietly.

CHAPTER 24

Daddy

• • •

"WAKE UP, LILY," ELI WHISPERED. "It's your birthday, baby girl."

Lily opened her sleepy eyes. "Morning, Daddy. Where's my surprise?"

"One-track mind," Eli grinned and tugged on her hair. "Put on some warm clothes and meet me in the kitchen."

Lily climbed carefully out of bed so she wouldn't wake up Zoe. Her sister's "friends" were lined up on the sides of the double bed they shared. Zoe had been collecting stuffed animals of every shape and kind for as long as Lily could remember. Each pet had a name and a particular place on the bed. Zoe didn't take kindly to anyone who messed up their order.

Lily didn't mind. She was thankful she wasn't the only girl in the house. Besides, Zoe was small and didn't take up too much room. Lily tucked the covers carefully around her sister. Zoe burrowed deeper beneath the thick quilt.

Lily gasped when her feet touched the cold wooden floor. It was winter, her favorite time of year. Not because it was the season of her birth, but because she loved playing in the snow more than anything. She took a deep breath, blowing a puff of steam into the air. She picked up the sweater and jeans she had thrown on the rocking chair in the corner and pulled them over her pajamas.

"Now, where are you?"

Looking around the room, then underneath the bed, she snatched her favorite pair of blue fuzzy socks from their hiding place. No time to waste, it was her birthday and there was a surprise waiting for her downstairs. Lily crept quietly out the door and down the hallway to Lucas' room.

He was sprawled across his bed with both feet hanging over the edge. Even though they were twins, you wouldn't have known it by their size. Lucas was all arms and legs, tall whereas Lily was petite. Lily shuddered as a cold blast of air swept through her brother's open bedroom window and out into the hall. Despite his serious and responsible nature, Lucas was always forgetting the little things, like turning out lights or putting the lid down on the toilet seat. Lily knew he did these things just to antagonize her. She knew the open window meant Lucas had spent his evening looking through his telescope, his Christmas present this year from their parents. Lucas spent countless hours staring at the sky, studying the stars and making model space rockets. He boasted to anyone who would listen that he was going to be an astronaut and soar into space one day or be a Jedi warrior who would save the world from the dark side.

Through Lucas' window, Lily watched big snowflakes fall in the grey morning light. Yippee! She would make snow angels today and she couldn't be happier. Lily tiptoed down the stairs and into the family kitchen, the heart of the Quinn household. Almost everything in the room had been designed and built by her father. The handcrafted pine table and chairs, the cuckoo clock on the wall that merrily chimed the hour and the large bench that collected everything that had no other place. Eli was a master craftsman. Her father had built their family home in the Colorado mountains, inside and out, as a labor of love.

Lily went to the back door and grabbed her pink coat from the hook on the wall. She pulled on her snow boots and dug through the pile of stuff on the bench for her hat and gloves. She knew this was going to be the best of all days. Anxious for her father, she donned her blue beanie and gloves and plopped on the bench to wait. That's when she saw it, the most wonderful thing in the world next to snow. Sitting in the middle of the kitchen table, looking delightful, was her favorite chocolate cake. Beside it was a strawberry cake, Lucas' favorite. Mia must have made them both last night after the twins had gone to bed. Lily practically jumped across the space to get to her cake.

Looking at the cake with longing, she decided that since her birthday had already officially begun she might as well have cake for breakfast. She lifted the glass lid carefully off the cake plate and stuck her finger right in the middle of the gooey chocolate icing.

"Lily Amanda! Stop right there," Eli exclaimed, zipping up his coat. "You can have your cake later. It's the first snow and I have a surprise for you and your brother."

"Lucas? He's coming?" Lily said with frustration.

"Well, it is his birthday too, young lady," Eli said.

"I'm here," Lucas laughed, sliding into the room jamming his hat on his head. "We can leave now."

"Let's go, you two," Eli ordered, holding out his big hands.

Hand in hand, Lily walked slowly with her daddy and Lucas through the newly fallen snow in their backyard. Into the forest of tall pine trees that surrounded their mountain home, they went. The cold snow stung her nose and caught in her dark lashes.

When they turned onto a familiar, well-worn trail, Lucas said, "I know where we're going."

"Yep, the clearing," Lily agreed. "What kind of wood are we looking for today, daddy?"

"Not sure, baby girl," Eli responded. "But, I'll know it when I see it."

"You always find just the right one," Lucas said proudly.

"Just like the both of you," Eli said. "Your mom and I were blessed when you were born. I'll never forget that day—both so tiny. I thought I might break you if I held you too tight."

"I love you daddy," Lily said squeezing his hand.

"All the way to the moon and back," Eli squeezed back.

"Me too," Lucas said seriously. "I even love Lily."

"As you should, little man," Eli answered. "Lily needs you—just like you need her. Y'all are a pair. You two have to take care of one another, always."

"And mom and Zoe, too," Lucas vowed.

Eli responded, "Strong and true we'll always be— "

"—full of love and happy you see," Lily added.

"Rain or shine, thick or thin," Lucas vowed.

"We won't give up, we're the Quinns!" they shouted together.

Lily looked up at her dad. Eli stopped and turned. His cheeks and nose were red above the stubble of a day's growth of beard. His dark brown hair, dusted with snow, fell across his brow and down his neck. His wide mouth fell easily into a smile and his clear green eyes, a match to Lucas', danced with amusement. He was a big teddy bear!

"I'll race you," Eli shouted. "Last one there is a rotten egg!"

Eli disappeared through a break in the trees. Lucas followed him, passing her up easily. She was the last one to the clearing. She loved this spot. It was a happy place for her family. In the middle of the space was a tree stump, knotted and gnarled. It was like her family's own little secret place in the middle of an enchanted forest. She had spent a lot of time here with them, picnics, storytelling, sing-a-longs and stargazing.

"Your old man has still got it! Beat ya fair and square!" Eli smiled.

"But I beat Lily!" Lucas shot back proudly.

"Betcha I can make a snow angel better than you," she boasted back.

She and Lucas fell into the snow to make the first snow angels of the winter. She jumped up, knowing her angel was so much better than her brother's. His design was just a mess of swishes in the powder. Hers, of course, was beautiful.

"See, mine's better. Look how big it is," Lucas exclaimed.

"It doesn't even look like an angel! It's just a big mess," she retorted.

"I don't know about you two, but I'm starving. Ready to head back for breakfast?" Eli asked.

"Yes!" she and Lucas answered together.

"I hope mom is making pancakes," she continued and grabbed Eli's hand.

Her stomach was growling loudly. One bite of chocolate icing hadn't—wait, a minute. "Daddy, what about our surprises? Did you forget?"

Eli grinned and patted the pocket of his jacket. "I was wondering if you would let me get by without giving you your gift."

"A promise is a promise," Lily said.

"Yes, it is," Eli agreed. "A man always keeps his promises, especially when he makes them to such a pretty girl."

She blushed, excited about what might be in Eli's pocket.

"Luc, get over here," she called. "It's time for our presents."

When Lucas didn't respond, Lily and Eli both turned around to find him standing motionless a few yards away.

"Come on Lucas, it's freezing out here," Eli called.

Lucas was white as a sheet. His lips were blue from the cold. His eyes were glazed over. Lily marched over to him and tugged on his arm.

"Stop, playing around, Luc," she said. "You're scaring me."

But Lucas didn't move. He didn't answer. Then, the demon angels with crimson hair and fiery blue eyes came. She was so frightened. A hooded man with a silver faceplate and a ruby ring approached her father. Lily felt her chest tighten, her windpipe constricted. It was all happening so fast. The man with the ruby ring was going to hurt her father. She knew it. She had to stop it. She flung herself at the man but was thrown back with the force of his blue flame. He reached up and removed his mask. But it wasn't Cain, it was Aiden. Her blood-curdling scream rent the cold air.

Then she was running with the other Light-bearers through the woods. They were scattered throughout the forest, moving in and out of the trees and dense underbrush. Celeste and Daniel were on either side of her. She heard Lucas shouting from behind her. He was urging her to quicken her pace. Something was chasing them. Faster and faster, she ran into the gloomy forest but the cold darkness was gaining. She knew if they didn't outrun the shadow, it would swallow them whole. Up ahead, Beni fell hard. Grotesque tree roots, black and gnarled, twisted around her friend. Pulled roughly into the dank earth, Beni disappeared. Lily and the others kept running. It was so very cold. It started snowing, heavy and fast, blinding her to everything. When she tripped and lost her balance, she screamed. She fell deep into the thick snow. Which way was up? Which way was down? Cold shards of ice stabbed her skin. Warm blood oozed from her arms and legs then congealed to a thin layer of red ice covering her body. She slammed into the hard ground. She lay there totally disoriented. Nausea roiled in her stomach. She swallowed back her vomit. Then, she heard them, low-pitched throaty growls coming from all sides. She opened her eyes. Flaming blue eyes slit in the frigid darkness. The beasts' menacing sounds declared their primal power and savagery, their hunger for blood. She was going to die.

"Not yet, my beauties," she hissed. "We want this poor girl to suffer a bit."

Lily knew that voice. It was Lysha, the woman who had murdered her father. Torches ignited, bathing the ice room in an amber glow. The beasts circled her, hissing and snarling.

Thunder rumbled, at first a violent crack, then a low rolling sound that shook the walls of ice. When they shattered, a woman clothed in a gown of deep sapphire stepped forth. It was her Aunt Scarlett.

"Silence!" Scarlett commanded.

Her voice sounded like a hollow wind in a deep cavern. The beasts were stilled and Lysha froze. Time stopped. The only thing moving was Scarlett's blood-red lips.

"The night is almost gone. The day is near when what is hidden will be revealed. Brothers will clash. Death will seize the one whose heart is not true. A promise fulfilled will bring forth the rise of hope."

Time moved again. Scarlett stepped back into the wall of ice and it closed around her. The beasts growled sharply, anxious to feed. Lily was on her own. She screamed when they pounced.

"Lily, wake up!" Jude shook her shoulders. "You're dreaming."

She opened her eyes but was paralyzed with fear. Her body damp with perspiration, her heart racing, she shivered, still feeling the deep cold in the room of ice.

"It was Aiden," she said brokenly. "I mean, it wasn't and then it was. The beasts were going to kill me, Jude. And Scarlett--I don't know what it all means."

"Did Scarlett say anything to you?"

"Yes, it was a prophecy. I'm sure of it."

"Then you need to write it down," Jude said handing her the small journal she kept by her bed.

Lily wrote down every detail of the prophecy and all she could recall from the dream.

"It will be light soon," Jude said. "You can tell everyone in the morning. Nolan will know what to do."

"Someone is going to die. The prophecy was clear, 'death will seize the one whose heart is not true.' And the brothers who clash—what if it's Jamie and Ioan? I'm afraid," Lily cried.

"You need to rest, Lily. Quiet your mind," Jude urged. "I'll watch over you."

"I don't want to dream anymore, Jude," Lily said, softly holding his hand. "It hurts too much."

"Let me ease your spirit," Jude said. He placed his hand on her hair and held it there. Immediately, she felt a wave of calm wash over her. She closed her eyes and drifted into a dreamless sleep.

CHAPTER 25

Trap

• • •

When Lily opened her eyes, she knew what she must do. She turned to Jude who was sitting in a chair beside her bed.

"What is it, Lily?" Jude asked.

"I keep dreaming about Daddy, our house, and what happened in the clearing the day he died, right?"

"Yes, the dream has come almost every night for two weeks now."

"What if Daddy is trying to tell me something? Show me something? Something I need to know for what is to come."

"Perhaps. It would make sense. But it might also just be a dream, Lily. You still grieve the loss of your father, and everything happening now just triggers those emotions in you even more."

"That's not it, Jude. The dream means something, especially now that it has been tied to the prophecy I received last night. I'm just missing it."

"You can speak with Nolan about it this morning. You must seek his wisdom."

"I have a better idea, but, you will have to help me do it."

"You know I will help you, always. But I know that look in your eyes. What are you planning?"

"I want you to take me back to our house in the mountains."

"No, not going to happen,"

"Wait a minute, hear me out. If I can just go back and be there, see the house, the clearing, I know I will figure out what the dream means. I need to do this, Jude."

"It's not safe. Scáths would attack us in moments. We can't go beyond the shield boundary."

"That's not true. You took me beyond the shield when we went to get Ioan and Jamie. You will protect me. Besides, we could take Celeste with us. She has grown so strong in her gift. If the Scáth do come, she could handle them. And you and Imani would be there as well. It's a good plan, Jude. Please."

"I don't like it, but if you believe going back will trigger the truth of the dream then you must do it. What if Celeste won't go?"

"Not to worry. She is fearless and ready to put her gift to use. She will come."

"Alright. But what about the others?"

"We will be there and back again before they miss us Jude. When we return, I will share the prophecy from the dream and whatever I find in the mountains."

"As you wish," Jude said. "Get Celeste. Imani and I will meet you at the crypt."

"Thank you, Jude," she said as she hugged him. "I hope you know how much this means to me—how much you mean to me. I couldn't face all of this without you."

"I know," Jude replied softly returning her embrace and then he left the room.

She pulled on her clothes, boots and a warm jacket. It would be cold in Colorado. There might even be snow. She smiled to herself. She hadn't seen snow in a long time. She knew her plan would work. There was something she was missing, and she would find it. When she found Celeste out on the back porch drinking a strong cup of coffee, it didn't take much to convince her to come along. Lily liked Celeste very much. She admired her even. In the short time she had known her, Lily had realized that Celeste was unfamiliar with anxiety and worry, Lily's constant companions. Celeste was confident, determined and had more courage in her little finger than Lily had in her whole body. Celeste was exactly who she needed to have her back today.

"Cher, I wouldn't miss this trip for the world," Celeste replied after Lily told her the plan. "I'm itching to get my hands on some demon scum."

She and Celeste met their angels at the crypt. Lily was still in awe of Celeste's guardian. Imani was magnificent and quite imposing with her sickle-bladed weapon.

"In and out, yes?" Imani asked. "Find what you need and be quick about it."

"Let's do this," Jude said.

The angels gathered Lily and Celeste in the safe haven of their wings and they were off.

The temperature dropped dramatically. When Lily's boots crunched in the snow, she knew she was back home. Her first glimpse of the cabin caused her to gasp. The crumbling walls were nothing more than a ghostly silhouette of some previous existence. Vivid memories of her happy life here flooded her. The passage of time and severe climate had not been a friend to the cabin nestled at the base of the mountain. The broken windows of her house stared back at her like the eyes of an empty soul.

"I'm going inside," Lily announced. "Celeste, come with me."

"Only a few minutes, Lily," Jude urged. "It's not safe here. Imani and I will watch the perimeter."

Lily walked up the stone steps to the front porch, Celeste following behind. The once beautiful wooden door, faded red and now rotten, hung loose on its hinges. She reached for the handle and turned it. The door creaked open slowly. Her footsteps echoed in the silence that hung heavy in the house.

"Someone has already been here," Celeste mused. "This place is a wreck."

"It must have been Cain and Lysha on the day they murdered my dad. They were looking for the saw, I bet."

"It's freezing in here," Celeste said.

She was right. Inside the cabin was dank and gloomy. Lily exhaled her breath in a puff of steam in the cold air. The interior of the house had been ransacked by wild animals or demons, or both. The overturned furniture, lovingly made by her father, was now decaying and frayed. All around were the artifacts of her life that her family had hastily abandoned that day so long ago. Lily moved deliberately, studying every corner, looking for some clue.

"What are we looking for?" Celeste asked.

"I'll know it when I see it," Lily said, echoing one of Eli's favorite phrases when searching for his precious wood.

"Hurry up! This place gives me the creeps—no offense. And I don't scare easy," Celeste said. "I'll check the kitchen."

"Ok, holler if you find something," Lily said.

Lily bent to pick up an old photo album. The brittle, yellowed pages still held images of her childhood. It crumbled in her hand just like her life had that day in December. In the corner of family room was a rocking chair, the only piece of furniture untouched and aright. She walked over to it. Sitting in the chair was a baby doll dressed in faded pink. It had been one of Zoe's dearest possessions. She picked it up and put it inside her jacket to take home to her sister. A crash in the kitchen startled her.

"Celeste? What's wrong?"

Lily bolted into the kitchen. Jude and Imani rushed in behind her alerted by her call.

Blue flaming cords shot from every corner of the kitchen, wrapping tightly around Jude and Imani. The floor opened up beneath them, and they were sucked below. Lily screamed. She was surrounded by Scáths. In the middle of the room, Lysha stood, arrogantly holding a leather leash.

"I gagged the dog," Lysha laughed.

Celeste's mouth was bound by a thick black leather muzzle preventing her friend's ability to speak. No wonder they had been overpowered. Gagged, Celeste had been unable to warn her or cast out the demons hissing around them. Lysha had been prepared and Lily had just walked them all into a trap.

"Checkmate," Lysha boasted.

"What did you do to Jude and Imani?"

"I've sent them far away, to the gates of hell to be exact. And there they will remain, for an eternity. Bound and helpless, suspended over the gates at the entrance to Gehenna. It is a nasty place, you know? They will be eternal greeters to the damned. I love the irony. My sweet pathetic Lily, your guardians can't help you now."

"You may have won this battle Lysha but you won't win the war," Lily swore with more bravado than she felt.

Lysha laughed again, "Poor Lily, we are going to win it all. Come now, Daddy is waiting."

Lily met Celeste's eyes. There was no fear there, just anger and determination. It gave Lily courage. She swallowed back her scream when the Scáths grabbed her roughly and the world exploded in blue.

CHAPTER 26

Rejection

• • •

AIDEN WATCHED THE CRACKLING FLAMES in the fireplace library. He wished he could jump into them and cleanse the torment from his mind and soul. He was being torn in two. He knew who and what he was. He had accepted his fate, even welcomed it. The evil that had swallowed him whole had become comfortable like a well-worn leather jacket. It fit. It all worked until a thought of her, a sweet memory, would break through, a small pinpoint of light in a wasteland of darkness.

He knew he could never lose her. That's why he had developed his plan—because of her—for her. His desire for her was unyielding. It drove him. He was one end of a string of fate connected to her. It bound him to her regardless of time, place or circumstance. His plan would require much. He would have to betray his father, his sister, and their legacy. He didn't know if he could do it, but he had to try. He couldn't imagine life without Lily. Yet, the fear of his father was just as compelling. He knew Cain had the power to sentence him to eternal damnation if he wanted. Aiden had wrestled night and day with this one question. Is fear more powerful than love, or is love the power that eclipses fear? He didn't know. But, he knew he would have to answer that question soon.

Lysha had promised to protect Lily. He wanted to believe his sister would keep her word but just in case, he had made a choice that would secure his control over Lily's fate. He had taken Simon's scroll to the diner and given it to Della for safekeeping. His family would never imagine that he would let the book out of his possession much less give it to someone like Della. Besides, Della didn't even know what she had, only that he had given her a backpack to keep for him until he came to retrieve it. She was to tell no one of their agreement. He knew he could trust Della, guileless and loyal. She had been like a second mother to him. If things got tight and didn't go his way concerning Lily, he would use the book as a bargaining chip. He knew his father and sister would never allow the book to be destroyed. It meant too much to both of them. It would be his and Lily's ticket to freedom. Once he exchanged the book for Lily, if she was ever caught or in danger, they would run far away and never look back.

"Don't you look just perfectly miserable? Like a cheesy Hallmark hero aching for his unrequited love?" Lysha drawled from the doorway. "I know just what will cheer you up!"

"Do tell, sister dear," Aiden said tiredly.

"Oooh, grumpy," she chided, sitting close to him on the leather couch. "I went hunting today and guess who I found?"

Aiden's worst fears were realized in that moment. His sister's comment awoke the serpents on his arms. He turned to her aghast.

"You guessed, didn't you?" Lysha said, noticing the slithering green serpents.

"Where is she?" he demanded. "I swear if you hurt her..."

"Aww, baby brother, did you forget the promise I made to you? Cause, I didn't," Lysha soothed. "Your sweet Lily is just fine. I put her down below for safekeeping until we figure out what to do with her."

"Why is she here? You know what father will do," Aiden said.

"I didn't plan it, you have to believe me, Aiden. I was after the one they call the Exiler. Her powers are the most dangerous to us. I had an opportunity, so I took it. I had no idea that Lily would be with her too. I figured I would bring her here, to you."

"What about Jude?" Aiden asked. "How did you separate Lily from her guardian?"

"It wasn't easy, believe me. I had to wait until just the right moment to make my move," Lysha smiled. "The Dìonadain is unable to help his precious Lily. He's hanging above the gates of Gehenna along with the one called Imani."

"You know you can't keep the Dìonadain bound forever, especially, not in Gehenna," Aiden scoffed. "Jude and Imani are probably on their way here now."

"We have time, brother," Lysha assured. "Andreas and his warriors will come for their own but, the army of demons I left behind will delay them I promise."

"Alright," he stood. "I'm going to get her and leave this place."

"I'm afraid it's too late for that now," Lysha whispered contritely.

"What do you mean, it's too late?"

"Father knows. He is on his way here already. K saw me and told father before I could stop him. Don't be mad," Lysha pleaded.

Aiden sat back down slowly. Nothing was going according to plan. Lily was here, a captive awaiting sure death. His father was on the way with only one goal in mind, the death of the Sorcha. And here he was. He didn't have Simon's book. He couldn't leave to get it now—he had no leverage.

"There will be other girls, I promise," Lysha assured.

"Of course, you're right," Aiden agreed. "But I wanted this one, sister."

He left the room, another plan, riskier than the first, forming in his tortured mind. He entered the elevator at the back of the house and plummeted stories below the mansion. The Talbot estate had been strategically built over a mammoth underground cave system. The doors opened and he stepped out. He took a flaming torch from its sconce on the stone wall. The cold damp air wrapped around him like a heavy coat of chain mail as he descended the tight spiral staircase into the bowels of the earth. Reaching the bottom, he was met by a series of Scáth sentries and guards. He drew his breath in deeply. Her scent was unmistakable. He followed it, knowing already where it would lead. He remained hidden just beyond the great stone wall separating him from her. His eyes, already accustomed to the darkness, looked for her. His fist tightened when he found her.

She was standing on the precipice of the great abyss. The natural rock walls of the cave encircled an unfathomably deep hole. Extending from the walls over the abyss were long thin protrusions or oubliettes. No gates. No bars. No locks. Just walls of air to imprison her. Lily was slumped against the rock wall behind her. Her head was bent, her beautiful blonde hair hung limply obscuring her face. Next to her was the Exiler. She was muzzled. His sister had meant business with this one. If the Exiler couldn't speak, then she couldn't thwart the movements of the Scáth or exile them to the kingdom of Gehenna. Thick iron chains embedded in the rock wall bound the Exiler's hands above her head.

Rao was hard at work taunting and torturing the Exiler. The former leader of his father's demon armies had been beaten and dethroned by his sister. Now that Lysha was the commander, Rao had been relegated to the position of Keeper of the Abyss. Rao exercised his fury and resentment over his defeat on whoever was unlucky enough to find themselves in his care.

Lily moaned. When she lifted her head, Aiden was furious. An ugly burn marred her face. Blood trickled from her mouth. Rao's handiwork, no doubt. If it had been anyone other than Lily, Aiden would have probably been entertained by Rao's torturous ways. But this was unconscionable.

"Enough," he thundered strutting around the wall and entering the outer edges of the abyss. Rao whirled around, angry at the intrusion.

"How dare you? The abyss is my domain. You don't give the orders here!"

"I said enough! You will obey me," Aiden commanded. "Don't test me, Scáth. I will throw you into the deepest recesses of your precious abyss if you refuse me."

"As you wish," Rao spat and slinked off.

Aiden looked first at Celeste who was watching him intently. Then he waved his hand. A walkway extended out in front of him allowing him to cross the abyss and reach Lily. She stared at him coldly. He could see the dislike clearly in her eyes, but, it didn't discourage him. He spied the tell-tale shaking of her leg, back and forth. She was anxious. She wasn't unmoved. She was conflicted about him. He would capitalize on that. He knew if he could just have a few minutes with her, rescue her and spirit her away, she would look at him like she had before, with love, admiration and hope. He reached out his hand and gently pushed her hair back from her bruised face.

"Don't touch me," she said passionately.

"I'm sorry, Lily. This is not what I wanted. You have to know I would never do anything to hurt you."

"You're a liar, Aiden. If you truly meant what you say, Celeste and I wouldn't be here right now."

"It's not that easy. You don't understand what I'm up against. My father—my sister."

"Don't pretend any of this is about them! You care for no one but yourself. You have proved that time and again."

"That's not true, Lily. I want a life with you. I need you. I don't care about light or dark. My allegiance is not to Abaddon, or Elohim, or even my father. It's to you."

"You only want me because you can't have me. I used to think there was good in you."

"Maybe there still is because of what I know I feel for you. It's real. I'm surrounded by darkness and I don't see a way out. You are my only lifeline. If you turn your back on me Lily, I will be lost forever."

"Look around you, Aiden. It's already too late. I'm chained to a wall and hanging out over the blackest pit I've ever seen. I've been tortured, and I'll probably die today. And you're just gonna stand there and watch, and cry, and tell me you're sorry and do nothing. The boy I loved, who loved me, is dead."

"Lily, you don't understand. I've been torn apart. The Aiden you knew is gone, that's true, but I had to destroy him so something of me could survive. The darkness in me overcame the light. Now I'm just numb—cold—desperately empty. I want to be free of this torture. Please help me?"

He reached for her hand. She jerked away from him.

"I'm not your savior, Aiden. Whatever we may have been, you destroyed it and there's no going back."

He bowed his head. He had lost her. He knew that now. His dreams of a future had only been the foolish fantasies of a misguided soul. He had made a choice, and the choice had cost him the only pure thing to ever touch his life besides his mother. He had failed both of them. He knew what he had to do. He lifted his head and his eyes flamed cold blue. Lily drew in a sharp breath.

"You're nothing but a coward! Do you hear me? A coward!" she yelled.

He turned on his heel and left her behind. Her screams echoing in his soul.

CHAPTER 27

Invitation

• • •

"How is this even possible?" Lucas demanded.

The Sorcha were gathered in the chapel, anxious and perplexed. When they couldn't find Lily or Celeste, searching both the house and the grounds of the campus, they had met back here to figure a plan of action.

"Jude and Imani must have taken them beyond the shield. It's the only thing that makes sense," Rafe answered.

"But why would they do that? They know the danger," Beni mused.

"I think I can answer that," Zoe said walking into the chapel carrying Lily's dream journal.

"Let me see it," Lucas said, reaching for the journal.

"Look at her last entry," Zoe urged.

Lucas studied his sister's handwriting, the words leaping off the page.

"What does it say?" Rafe asked.

"She had a dream about the day Dad was murdered—then it gets real jumbled—lots of darkness, Aiden and terrifying beasts. She was given a prophetic word, though. It says, 'the night is almost gone. The day is near when what is hidden will be revealed. Brothers will clash. Death will seize the one whose heart is not true. A promise fulfilled will bring forth the rise of hope.'

"Well, that's real pretty, but what does it mean?" Ioan asked.

"Only Lily could tell us that, but it still doesn't explain where they went or why," Lucas returned.

"Yes, it does," Zoe answered. "Turn the page, Lucas."

Lucas did and read aloud. "I know my dreams of Dad mean something. There has to be a clue I'm missing somewhere. I'm going back."

"Back where?" Ariel asked.

"Our house in Colorado," Lucas said.

"Well, let's go," Jamie said excitedly. "We have to get them."

The chapel doors swung wide. "I'm afraid the ones you seek are no longer there," Nolan said, ominously striding down the aisle. "Bring in the Scáth."

Kiefer and Ira escorted a Scáth messenger into the chapel. He was not bound, walking forward of his own free will. His crimson hair hung in braids down his back. He was clothed in silver, his leathered wings folded behind him.

"Deliver your message," Nolan thundered.

The Scáth turned his smoldering eyes on Lucas and hissed, "My master cordially extends an invitation to the House of Quinn."

Lucas reached for the parchment envelope in the messenger's hand. He broke the red wax seal and read the message inside.

"It is with great pleasure and the highest esteem that I extend this invitation. Please join me and my family for a celebratory dinner tonight at 7pm. We have much to discuss. Black-tie required. Let's make it grand, shall we? And be punctual—I don't like to wait. Ever yours, C."

Lucas' hand trembled with barely restrained anger. "You've done what you came to do, now, get out!"

The messenger hissed, "As you wish. What should I tell my master?"

"Tell him we're coming, and Lily and Celeste better not be harmed."

The messenger nodded his head and was then escorted back out by the Dìonadain.

"It's a trap, you can't go," Ariel said.

"Come on, man, don't you see this is what he wants? He wants to make us even more vulnerable than we already are," Ioan added.

"I have an uneasiness in my spirit. It's not going to go well if you go tonight," Daniel urged.

"We have no choice," Lucas said. "I'm not leaving Lily or Celeste there."

"If Cain wanted to stop the uniting, he would have already killed them both," Wei suggested. "He's the commander of the demon armies. This dude is the ultimate evil. Something doesn't add up."

"She's right. Cain wants something else," Rafe agreed.

"Yeah, but what?" Jamie interjected.

"What do you think, Nolan?" Lucas turned to his guardian, the one he trusted above all others.

"Cain is a playing a game of chess. Unfortunately, Lily and Celeste are his pawns. The only way to know for sure what Cain wants is to make a move of our own."

"Meaning we have to go," Zoe said.

"We must let the evening unfold. All is not known. However, all is not lost," Nolan said.

"I'm betting on Cain's greed and pride being bigger than his need to kill and destroy."

"Translation, please."

"Cain wants to capture all of us—the ultimate trophy—more than he wants to destroy us. It's his weakness," Lucas explained.

"None of this talk matters. We have to rescue Lily and Celeste. We can't let them die," Wei said.

"What can we do, Lucas? To help?" Ioan asked.

"Pray. It's all we can do, now," Lucas responded.

"Our prayers will strengthen you, Lucas. They will encourage you, Zoe," Daniel said. Elohim will hear our prayers. He will guide you, protect you. We must not lose faith now. Remember what John said to Asher. They must be immovable in their faith when they are tested. This is our test," Daniel said.

"Zoe, we need to go back to the house and change. We only have an hour. We can't risk being late," Lucas said. Turning to the rest of the group, he said, "We will bring them home, I promise."

He and Zoe ran back to the house.

"Meet you back here in 30 minutes, yes?"

"I won't be late," Zoe leaned up and kissed him on the cheek. "I'm proud of you Luc. I'm really glad you're my brother."

With that simple declaration of her faith in him, Zoe ran up the stairs to her room. Lucas, his mind laser-focused, walked to his. Black-tie? What a ridiculous request! He pulled out the suit he had worn to the Museum Gala months before. He would dress the part. Far be it from him to disappoint! When he walked out of his room, he was surprised to see Mia standing with Zoe at the bottom of the stairs. His mother was dressed in an elegant black dress with a single strand of pearls shining at her neck. The look on her face was resigned.

"You're not going without me. The invitation was addressed to the House of Quinn and the last time I checked, I was the head of that house," Mia announced.

"Mom, it's too dangerous," Lucas said.

"This is not a negotiation, Lucas," Mia said. "Not another word. We need to focus on getting your sister back."

Lucas and his family walked out the front door to find Nolan, Tov and Asher waiting on them. It was a somber, determined group. The road ahead was unknown, fraught with many dangers and possible snares. Once they left the sacred ground of Centenary, they would be completely vulnerable and exposed. There would be no turning back.

"So, it is written, when you sit down to eat with a ruler, consider who and what are before you. For you will put a knife to your throat if you are a man given to desire. Be not desirous of his sweets, for it is deceitful food offered with questionable motives," Nolan warned.

"Cain has nothing I could ever want, accept my sister and our friend," Lucas said.

"Yes, Cain knows that, Luc, and he will use it against you, and for his own gain," Mia responded. "Be alert, my children," she said, caressing each one's face. "Into the lion's den we go."

Before his feet left the ground, Lucas caught sight of his friend, on his knees in the grass, his hands extended toward the heavens.

"Yea, though I walk through the valley of the shadow of death, I will fear no evil," Daniel prayed.

Lucas allowed his friend's words to sear his heart and mind. He would not allow fear and faith to co-exist in his heart. He was a Light-bearer, and he was going to act like it.

They landed softly on the front lawn outside the Talbot mansion. The house was lit up like a Times Square on New Year's Eve. Lucas led his family to the front door. He rang the bell. It was opened by the butler, Thomas.

"Welcome, Master Quinn, ladies," Thomas said in his clipped English accent. "Please come in. Wait just there in the foyer."

Lucas noticed Thomas' total disdain for their Dìonadain guard, never acknowledging their presence, although it was quite spectacular.

"I'm nervous, and this is eerie. It's like this is supposed to be just a normal dinner party with the rich and famous," Zoe whispered, linking her hand in his.

"I think I hear the Eagles singing *Hotel California*," Lucas grinned easily, doing his best to calm his sister's nerves.

"My favorite family, I'm so happy you could join us this evening," Cain announced as he sauntered down the grand staircase.

Following him were his children, Lysha, striking in an emerald green silk gown, Kayanja, in his customary stark white suit, and Aiden, nonchalant and arrogant in his fitted black dinner jacket and open-collar white shirt. Lucas only smelled death coming his way. Cain, no longer masquerading as Flynn Talbot, a master of style and class, couldn't cover his putrid stench. Interesting, Aiden and his siblings, the Mescáths, had no distinct scent at all. It was the glowing green serpents, writhing up and down their arms and necks, that repulsed Lucas. There was no beauty in any of them.

"And Mia, my sweet, what a pleasant surprise," Cain said smoothly. "Come my honored guests. Dinner is waiting."

Lucas and his family followed the Talbots into the dining room. It was a spectacular study in ruby red and gold. Heavy drapes covered the tall French windows. An ornate mahogany table graced the center of the room. Gorgeous crystal chandeliers hung over the table. Candelabras, dripping with wax, adorned the fireplace mantle as well as the massive chiffoniere. A gorgeous oil painting of Lysha, Aiden, Kayanja and Cain hung over the marble fireplace, its carved serpents writhing in bas-relief. A fire roared, but the room was untouched by its warmth. Beethoven's *Moonlight Sonata* filled the room. Lucas didn't know where the music was coming from, but it didn't matter; it was all a play, a farce, put on for their benefit.

"Please sit," Cain admonished. "You will find your name card at your seat. Nolan, the Dìonadain are not welcome at my table. You'll wait outside."

"He will not," Lucas said forcefully. "Our guardians stay with us."

"As you wish," Cain conceded. "I have ordered an exceptional prime rib for our pleasure. I hope you like your meat rare."

"I don't eat meat," Zoe said smartly.

Aiden grinned. It infuriated Lucas.

"Let's just cut to the chase, shall we?" Lucas suggested. "You know what we want. The question is, what do you want?"

"Patience, young man. I'll decide when we talk business. For now, we are going to enjoy a lovely family dinner."

"You're crazy," Zoe spouted. "You're holding my sister and my friend captive, who knows where, and God only knows what you've already done to them. And you want me to eat dinner?" Zoe spouted.

"Rest easy, little Zoe. Lily and Celeste are unharmed, just as long as you and your family cooperate," Cain ordered. "Mia, I would have thought a child of yours would have better manners. Tsk, tsk. My children never speak without my leave. Isn't that right, Aiden?"

"Yes, father," Aiden responded.

Lucas stared him down but Aiden refused to meet his eyes. Dinner was served. Lucas pushed his food around on his plate. His senses were in overdrive. The scent of death mixed with the smell of rare meat wafting about the room made him want to vomit. The shadow of evil pressed in on him like a vice. He felt like his bones were literally going to pop out of his skin. He was having difficulty focusing. His heightened senses were bombarded and offended on every level at this table of pure evil. He willed himself to be patient, to wait Cain out. The conversation was one-sided and droned on. Cain boasted about his infamous past, hunting and killing generations of Sorcha. When dessert was removed from the table, the tension in the air shifted. Finally! Now, he would find out exactly what they were up against and what they would have to do to get Lily and Celeste back.

Cain wiped his mouth delicately with his linen napkin and sat back from the table, crossing his legs casually. "Now, I'm ready to talk business. There will be no negotiation, only destruction or compromise if you are unwilling. Do you understand?"

Lucas nodded his head, his eyes never leaving Cain's.

Cain continued, "You want your sister and Celeste returned to you. This is not something that benefits me. All I have to do is end either of their lives and the hope for a uniting in this generation is obliterated. I win. You lose. But I have decided that their lives, your lives, can benefit me if you are willing to compromise."

"I'm listening," Lucas said quietly.

"I am in need of more children. I like big families."

"What are you asking me?"

"Don't be obtuse, Lucas. You know exactly what I am asking. I will allow Lily to live if you will give your mother to me. I will care for her. She will want for nothing."

"Not a chance," Zoe cried. "You are a cruel man."

"I am not a man, you ignorant, girl!" he said disdainfully. "I am Cain, fallen angel and commander of the Scáths. I am highly favored by my Prince and wield so great a power you cannot fathom it. How dare you compare me to a man?"

"I'll do it," Mia said. "Promise me you will leave my children be. You will never see them or touch them again."

"Mom, you don't know what you're saying," Lucas said.

"It's the only way, Luc, to save Lily," Mia assured.

"Your mother is right, Lucas," Cain urged. "Listen to her. In return, you will have your sister back. And I vow to leave the rest of you alone."

"What about Celeste?" Lucas asked. "Does she go free as well?"

"You know better than that, Lucas. I can never allow the Sorcha to unite. Celeste will have to die. Remember, I told you from the beginning you would have to compromise."

"I can't allow it," Lucas whispered.

"You really have no choice. Think on it. I expect an answer in twelve hours, no more, no less. If you don't bring Mia to me then, both Lily and Celeste will die. Now, get out of my house. You are no longer welcome here."

He had no time to respond. The Dìonadain grabbed them and spirited them away into the night.

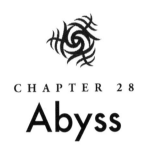

CHAPTER 28

Abyss

• • •

"That went rather well, don't you think?" Lysha suggested.

"Perfect in every way, my sweet," Cain agreed. "Lucas has no choice. He will wrestle with the decision. But, he will make it."

"How can you be so sure, father?" Kayanja asked.

"He is his father's son. Eli would have sacrificed the one to save the many. It's the way of the Light-bearer. Besides Mia will never let her daughter die. She will come tonight."

"Why her? Why is Mia so special?" Aiden asked.

"You're under her daughter's spell, you should know," Lysha jabbed.

Aiden had walked into his sister's trap. He knew nothing would anger his father more than to know his son was still struggling with feelings for Lily Quinn. He wasn't wrong.

"I told you to be done with that girl," Cain said menacingly.

Aiden met his father's harsh look with one of his own.

"I am. Lysha is mistaken. Lily Quinn has no power over me. She is a plaything and nothing more."

"Good," Cain drawled, his face relaxing. "Very good. My children, it's time we pay our guests a visit."

Aiden didn't care for the nonchalant tone in Cain's voice. He knew more was going on here tonight than he had realized. He felt his rage, the raw emotion he battled to keep in check, begin to simmer. He didn't like being pushed into a corner. His desire for Lily was at odds with everything else in his life that made him who he was. And she didn't even want him, she hated him. What was he even fighting for? He made a decision as he rode with his family down the long elevator shaft to the caverns below. He was done with Lily Quinn. Her fate was out of his hands.

When the elevator doors slid open, Aiden realized his father had not been entirely truthful upstairs. They weren't the only visitors to the abyss. There were Scáths milling about everywhere. The air was rife with anticipation, an insatiable hunger for death. Familiar yet hideous chants sounded in the distance. If there was one thing his father loved it was a spectacle, a public show of torture and death which assaulted the senses and ratcheted up emotions. Cain had ordered the construction of viewing stands encircling the abyss so his minions could enjoy a show whenever his father fancied it. The massive space resembled the grand Coliseum of Rome, where gladiators fought to the death and Christians were devoured by lions in ancient times.

Aiden joined his father on the grand viewing platform situated two stories above the abyss. Lysha and Kayanja sat on either side of their father, the right and left hand of evil. He stood just behind his father's seat over Lysha's right shoulder, not because he was the youngest but because he had not yet earned the right to sit beside his father. He would have to fight for that privilege, literally. Aiden could only secure a coveted position beside Cain if he challenged either of his siblings in hand-to-hand combat and won.

Aiden spared a glance at the two Light-bearers below. Chained to the rock wall, battered and bruised, they must have realized that death was coming for them both. There would be no rescue, no reprieve. Lily and Celeste, who was still muzzled, looked resigned to their fate, brave even. He admired their courage, obviously holding on to the possibility of a rescue. But Aiden knew there would be none. Aiden knew neither had any idea what was coming for them. If they had, there would be nothing but fear on their countenances. The abyss was home to the behemoth, the most terrifying horror Aiden had ever seen. A primordial beast of enormous strength and proportion who existed in the deep recesses of the earth. This monster of chaos, once unleashed, was beyond the control of man or demon until it was satisfied with human flesh.

"You're going to kill them? What about the compromise you made with Lucas?" he whispered to his father.

"I lied," Cain smiled. "Tonight, my son, I win. I will conquer the Sorcha and destroy Nolan's chance of uniting them for this generation. And I get Mia, an extraordinary woman of spirit, as my companion, for as long as I want her."

His father's chilling smile was one he knew all too well. Aiden knew Cain fancied himself to be emperor of an ancient time, a time fraught with spectacle, death, and torture, all for the cheering masses. He found joy in power, in dominating, in making others subservient to his will. Cain's desire to be a showman, to entertain not only himself but the legions of Scáth under his command, had motivated him to build this arena as well as several others in his strongholds around the globe. His father's cruelty was driven by his insatiable need for two things only: fame and power.

Tonight, Lily and her friend Celeste would be the main attraction.

Cain stood and addressed the chanting masses.

"My brothers and sisters, before you stand two Light-bearers, spawn of Elohim, the Creator, children of Yeshua, the Light. They, and their comrades, seek to destroy us, to wipe the earth clean of our presence. But they have failed. We are more powerful. We have dominion. The Scáth will not be destroyed. Tonight, join me in the sweet taste of victory. Let us celebrate with their blood and their agony!"

The Scáth screamed and hissed with delight. Lysha and Kayanja cheered. Aiden was silent. He didn't know if he could watch Lily die. He knew it was her fate. Lily had said it best. She was light. He was dark. The boy she had loved was dead. He was a monster, like his father, like the beast of the abyss. He hoped her death, letting go of her light, would make him stronger. Besides, he had the thrill of the hunt, the satisfaction of destroying flesh. No more voices in his head telling him he couldn't live without her, no more positive force demanding he be good. Only darkness—alone, and in complete control, he would no longer feel empathy or guilt for who he was and what he would do. But he couldn't watch. He backed away quietly, hoping he wouldn't be missed.

"My son," Cain said deliberately, never turning around. "You will stand with me. It's time to put your convictions to the test."

Aiden cringed inwardly but showed no emotion at his father's request. He obeyed without objection. His worst fear came true, he would have to watch Lily Quinn die. The internal struggle he felt gripped his gut and twisted it painfully. Could he do it?

"Call the beast!" Cain commanded.

A drum, sounded by Rao, called the behemoth from the depths of the abyss. The crowd went wild. Up from the darkness came the glow of two yellow eyes, like sallow lamplight. The closer it got, the faster Aiden's heart beat in his chest. He spared a glance at Lily. He could see the fear widening her eyes. Celeste was struggling against her chains. They didn't have a chance.

Out of the great void it came. Two legs like towers of iron, a muscular torso hard and lean, a long tail stiff and massive like a cedar tree, two arms with razor-sharp claws and fangs the size of a man's arm, feral yellow eyes and a furry ridge running from its head across its back that would fire a deep crimson when the savage creature roared. Four-thousand-pounds of dense muscle, claws and fangs, and it wanted fresh meat. It moved with great stealth and grace for its size. A gelatinous saliva dripped from its wide mouth onto the dirt of the area floor. It roared with such great savagery, it silenced the cavernous space. The beast eyed its prey, chained and vulnerable, standing on the oubliette. Aiden knew the monster was more like a cat than a snake. Instead of killing fast, it preferred to toy with its food. It would be a slow death. All eyes were trained on the ghastly beast. Except for Aiden's—he met Lily's eyes across the torch-lit expanse.

Aiden made his choice, one he had known in his soul that he always would. In an instant, he was laser-focused. He had a job to do. Save Lily and her friend. He jumped from the balcony, where his family was watching the terror unfold, onto the oubliette below. He fired two blue darts at Lily's chains and then Celeste's. They fell away from their wrists. He heard his father roar in the distance, but, he ignored it. Shielding Lily and Celeste, he turned to face the beast.

A litany of curses unraveled from his tongue as the creature advanced. Every step the behemoth took rattled Aiden's bones. The beast was angry now. Aiden stood between it and its prize. Aiden dodged a swing from the beast's massive claw. He pummeled the beast with a lightning round of blue darts. The beast roared and renewed its bloodthirsty attack. Aiden tumbled off the oubliette and into the narrow ring of dirt circling the pit, leaving Lily open to attack. Using all his strength, Aiden jumped on the beast's head and swung his body around hard, placing the beast in a chokehold. The beast turned away from the oubliette. It reached up, dragging Aiden off and casting him to the ground. The force knocked all the breath out of Aiden. The beast struck Aiden's side with one of its massive clawed arms. Blinding pain seared through his gut. He closed his eyes. He had fought valiantly, but he had failed her. He could hear nothing now—no hisses from the audience, no roars from the creature, no rhythm from the beating drum, just silence. Everyone poised for the deathly blow that would signal his end. He looked up at Lily one last time. She was smiling. Did she welcome his death? She held her friend's leather muzzle in her hand. And then the voice came, shouting with authority, echoing throughout the arena.

"In the holy name of Yeshua, the Light, I command you, oh legion of demons, to come out of this man," Celeste spoke.

Aiden lost all sense of time and space. His body convulsed violently on the hot ground. He felt his chest explode. The darkness that had so long filled him, plagued him, rushed out in one violent surge. The behemoth stalked toward him ready to rip his flesh. His last coherent thought was of the pure peace he felt pulsing through him.

"Please, Elohim, save them for I could not," he whispered brokenly.

The ground shook violently. A golden hot light burst from above. The glorious Dìonadain warrior, shield and spear in hand, landed heavily in front of Aiden. His mighty wings flapped vigorously, sending swirls of dust into the behemoth's mouth and eyes. The beast choked and fell back. The Dìonadain advanced. With one hand, he closed the mouth of the beast binding it shut with the force of the Light.

"I am Ehud, the guardian of the Leader of the Sorcha. You will not harm him," the warrior thundered to all in the arena.

Aiden rubbed the back of his ear trying to still the tingling sensation he felt there. It must be the mark—just like the one he had seen behind the Irishman's ear in the fighting cage months ago. He was unsure of what had just happened to him. The only thing he knew was that he was free. The evil within him was gone, its shadow no longer residing in his soul, cast out by the Exiler, Celeste. Aiden looked up toward his father who was standing on the grand parapet. Cain's perfect features were contorted in a mask of shocked fury. Lysha lunged suddenly, her eyes flaming blue. Aiden knew his sister must have been filled instant hatred towards him at the Ehud's revelation. She probably wanted nothing more than to strike him down where he stood. Cain jerked her back and wrapped her in his dark wings. Aiden knew at that moment he would be forever separated from his family.

Aiden gained his footing. He had to get them all out of here. Before he could take another step, he was knocked down forcefully from behind. It was Kayanja. His brother's lethal skills were legendary. He was a master assassin, after all. Even though Aiden had always hated K, he respected his brother's ability as an assassin and had been smart enough to never challenge him to a physical fight. Now, the playing field had been dramatically altered. Aiden no longer hated K, but pitied him. Brothers would now clash, a duel between light and darkness. Aiden felt a strength he had never known before. He turned to his brother.

"It doesn't have to end like this, K," he pleaded.

"Yes, it does," K responded, releasing a dozen short bursts of blue flame from his palms.

Aiden was driven back. Burns covered his arms and face. He had no weapon to defend himself with.

"You're pathetic," K said calmly. "I always knew you weren't worthy of father's favor."

Again, K pummeled him with fiery darts. Aiden's body was screaming with pain, but he had a plan. Closer and closer, he retreated back to the abyss. K, enjoying his brother's torture, continued to advance. Kayanja spit in the dirt. Deliberately, he removed the leather strap from the saw he wore on his back. He held it up before Aiden and brandished it like a weapon. He stuck the point of the saw in the dirt and flexed both hands. He was amping up to deliver a deadly onslaught.

"I am going to kill you, Light-bearer. And then I am going to saw your body in half just like father did when he took Simon's life. Your death will be my victory—the saw my trophy."

"Come and get me then," Aiden taunted. He was crouched at the very edge of the abyss.

When Kayanja closed the short distance between them, Aiden kept his body low. He rolled to the right, grabbed the saw and shouted, "Ehud, now!"

Ehud loosed the mouth of the beast. The behemoth leapt toward the abyss. Kayanja turned from the edge of the abyss too late. The beast grabbed K in its powerful jaws cracking his body in his powerful mouth. He dove into the depths of the black hole, taking Kayanja with him.

He heard Lysha's shout of disbelief. The Scáths' high-pitched screams of fury followed those of his sister. They bombarded Aiden. He stood to his feet, his guardian radiant beside him. The ground trembled. A sound like a rushing wind filled the space. Eleven shafts of golden light landed around him. Twelve Light-bearers stood, their guardians resplendent in gold behind them. The Dìonadain had buried their golden broadswords in the earth, creating a shield around the twelve. Slowly, Aiden met the eyes of each person in the circle who had just moments ago been his enemy. The two people that mattered the most couldn't have been more opposite in their reaction to his newfound role. Lily was smiling at him, tears of joy welling in her eyes. Lucas, however, just stared. There was respect in his glance but not acceptance. Aiden knew he would have to earn that from his friend.

His choice for love, for Lily, for Elohim, had changed his life forever. He was the Leader of the Sorcha, a Light-bearer chosen and gifted by Elohim, the Creator of all things. He was the last link in a chain that could not be broken. The circle was complete, the prophecy fulfilled. The Sorcha would now unite the Light within them to destroy the darkness in this world.

"The light shines in the darkness, and the darkness has not overcome it!" Nolan roared.

Twelve Light-bearers joined hands forming an infinite circle of light. A terrible rumble from deep in the belly of the earth sounded. The ground began to move as if it were a wave on the sea. The rock walls, which had stood for centuries, cracked and crumbled. The Scáths scattered wildly, flying all about the space. Within the circle Aiden felt only peace and power. Outside it, he knew there was chaos. The horrifying shrieks of the demons who were trying to flee bounced off the pulsing shield of protection. He looked for Cain and Lysha amid the pandemonium, but they were nowhere to be found.

Suddenly, Aiden felt a volcano of energy well up within him. It consumed his mind, body and soul. There was nothing but pure light. He had never felt anything like it before. He knew the same thing must be happening to the others in the circle. Thousands of years in the making, the uniting of the Light would now take place. The tremendous worth of the many sacrifices and deaths of Light-bearers throughout the ages would now be realized. Darkness would not win this day. When the great light burst forth from the twelve, it joined them and surrounded them. There were three massive pulses of energy and then a sonic boom leveled everything.

CHAPTER 29

Watchmen

• • •

THE CHARGED ATMOSPHERE IN THE Hall of the Sorcha was palpable. The twelve Light-bearers sat in their carved stone seats in front of the likenesses of their forebears. Still reeling from the after-effects of the uniting, Lucas sat withdrawn and confused. His enemy was now his brother, a warrior of the Light, just as he was. Lucas struggled with the reality of the situation now. He would have to follow Aiden, allow him to lead, to guide the others. Lucas didn't like it.

How were they supposed to trust Aiden? He had tried to kill them. Just hours ago, before Celeste had cast the evil from him, Aiden had been a Mescáth, an assassin who preyed upon the Light. But now, Aiden had a pure heart, one full of hope and purpose. His mother had been a Light-bearer, so that meant something to Lucas. Yet he couldn't look at Aiden now and not expect his eyes to flame blue at any moment. The aura of evil around Aiden was no longer there. Lucas could sense that. But, there was still so much to be resolved. Although Aiden had made a choice for the Light, Lucas knew he would now have to dedicate his life to its purpose. Would Aiden be willing to give his allegiance to Elohim no matter the cost?

Still, Lucas wrestled with the reality of Aiden's position in the twelve now. It wasn't jealousy. He was confident, assured in his gift as the Perceiver. He never imagined himself the Leader. He had always known that the Leader would emerge. But the last person he ever imagined it would be was Aiden. It was just a complete lack of trust in Aiden, as well as a lack of understanding of why Elohim would have chosen someone so horrible to lead their quest. It hadn't taken Aiden long at all to embrace the mantle of leadership. He wore it well, Lucas had to admit, and the others seemed to have accepted him readily enough even Wei and Rafe, who had been in that tunnel in New York and witnessed the evil of Aiden Talbot. He wondered if Lily was struggling with the same thoughts. But all of that would have to wait. The Light-bearers could not take another step without the map to guide their way.

The saw lay on a raised dais in the center of the circle. Thus far, they had not been able to figure out the meaning of the etchings that covered the blade. Beni had tried but had ascertained it was not a language. Then Rafe had marshalled the strength of his mind to tackle the riddle of the saw. But, again, it was beyond his intellect to decode it. Celeste had even commanded the truth of the saw to be revealed but nothing had happened. So here they sat, frustrated, impatient and at a loss.

"What does it matter? Even if we could understand the map on the saw, we don't have Simon's book!" Lucas interjected into the silence.

Lucas and Ioan had gone with Aiden to retrieve the book after the uniting. Aiden had left Simon's scroll, hidden in a backpack, in Della's care at the diner. But when they had asked Della for it, she had had no memory of Aiden ever giving it to her. They had searched the diner but the backpack was not there. Lucas figured it was probably now in the hands of Cain or Lysha, both of whom had mysteriously disappeared in the chaos and demolition caused by the uniting.

"We will find Simon's book, Luc. I promise you that," Aiden vowed.

"What if your father or sister have it?" Lucas demanded.

"There's no way! Neither of them had any idea of what I had done with the book or who I had given it to," Aiden responded.

"I hope you're right," Lucas returned, leaning back in his seat frustrated. "Daniel, would you pray for Aiden? We need Elohim to give him wisdom, he is our Leader, after all."

Lucas figured his sarcasm was not lost on the group when Daniel stood up and walked to the center of the circle.

"We need Elohim to guide Aiden in what He would have us all to do, Lucas," Daniel said with solemn authority. "Elohim has chosen him as our Leader, it is not our place to argue with His will.

Daniel knelt on the stone floor and asked Aiden to join him there. Although, Lucas was skeptical about Aiden's sincerity at this point, he was completely trusting in Daniel's ability to move the heart of Elohim through prayer. Daniel began to pray. Lucas was stunned when a human hand, glowing faintly with light, appeared immediately in the air behind Aiden. The others must have shared his sentiment if their swift indrawn breaths were any clue. The fingers of the hand wrote with fire on the face of the stone pedestal beneath the statue of the Leader. The message, whose meaning was unknown to Lucas, burned in the stone. The hand hovered in the air when the message was complete.

"Look, Aiden, behind you," Zoe cried.

Aiden turned around. Lucas watched Aiden's face drain of color and his limbs tremble at the sight of the hand and the flaming message before him. As immediately as it had appeared, the hand was gone. Aiden sat there, studying the message left behind. Lucas knew that the Leader was gifted with not only a strategic mind and courageous spirit for battle, but that he also heard directly from Elohim. As the Leader, Aiden would be able to converse directly with Elohim and receive His wisdom and guidance.

"I have heard your plea, Leader, and my Spirit is in you. Receive my wisdom. The saw, when possessed by all, will reveal what has been hidden guiding you to your path," Aiden announced slowly.

"What does that mean?" Lily asked.

"Everyone come to the saw," Aiden directed.

Lucas joined the others standing around the saw.

"What now?" he urged, unable to deny the divine revelation of the flaming message and Aiden's obvious role now in their group.

Aiden placed his hand on the saw and said, "Everyone touch the edge of the saw."

All twelve laid a hand on the saw's blade. The etchings burst with light and began to move. The lines and curves, once only incoherent squiggles, joined in the center of the saw to form the undeniable sign of the Sorcha, bright and bold.

"Oh, my goodness, look at that?" Lily exclaimed. "It's beautiful."

"But I still don't see a map. How are we supposed to know where we are going?" Lucas asked.

"I will take you," a voice boomed from the entrance to the chamber.

Lucas looked up, startled. Who was this woman? And better yet, how did she get in here? Only the Dìonadain and Sorcha were allowed in this hallowed hall.

"Sephra, you have traveled far, my friend. Welcome," Nolan announced before embracing the woman.

The woman Nolan called Sephra was of ordinary height and a slight yet well-muscled build. Her dark hair was braided and tied back from her angular face. Her watchful gray eyes were serious like a hawk. She was dressed in dark fitted trousers, shirt, boots and a loose-fitting coat.

Sephra strode purposefully toward them. She stopped and bowed her head in a show of deference to the twelve. What did that mean? Lucas had thought he was beyond surprises; but this woman, with her unexpected arrival, obvious camaraderie with Nolan, and her weirdly common yet ancient clothing and hairstyle unsettled him.

"Who are you?" Aiden asked curtly.

"My beloved Sorcha, I am your guide, Sephra of the Natsar, descendant of Ahmlaid, son of Simon. I have been sent to bring you home. For thousands of years, we have been watching and waiting, preparing for you. The uniting has made you powerful. You have been shown ready and equal to the tasks that lie ahead. It is now time for our journey."

"You will take us to the key?" Lucas asked.

"I will take you to the stronghold of the Natsar, the watchmen on the tower. The rest you will have to earn. Your journey will be long and the trials set before you will require a sacrifice from each of you, one that will surely test your resolve and the bond that now ties you all tightly together. Time is of the essence. Abaddon will stop at nothing to prevent you from reading the book and learning the secret to his destruction."

"Yeah, well, that's where we have a slight problem," Aiden responded. "I had the book. But I made a risky choice and gave it to someone for safekeeping. I was wrong to think it would be protected out of my possession. Now, it's gone, disappeared into thin air."

"Do not dismay, Light-bearers," Sephra said, pulling Aiden's backpack from beneath her coat. "I thought it would be better if the book was in my care for a time. Now, I give it back to you. Guard the book, no matter what."

Aiden took the backpack from Sephra and slung it over his shoulder. "I'll never let it out of my hands again," he assured.

"Gather your things, Light-bearers. Time waits for no one."

Everything was happening so fast. Lucas felt like he was on a bullet train into the unknown. He grabbed the saw and strapped it to his back for safekeeping. The Dìonadain guardians sheltered the twelve within their wings and prepared for flight. Lucas realized that finding each other, learning to use their gifts, uniting the Light, was all just the start of an epic purpose that lay ahead of them. He was ready—they all were. Rushing up into the starry sky, Lucas knew the Sorcha's quest had just begun.

Epilogue

• • •

The journey that lay ahead would not be easy
Challenge and peril will be our constant companions.
There is no safe way where we are going.
But, what else can we do?
We were chosen.
Twelve strangers, hunted and haunted by tragedy, but a family now.
We are the Sorcha.
Warriors who wield great powers of the Light.
When we first received our gifts, we didn't understand them.
We know now what we are capable of.
We will stand and fight.
Our destiny is written but our fate is still unclear.
It no longer matters who we were, only what we must do.
The real battle has just begun.
You see, no one else had ever made it this far
It's up to us now.
Funny, aren't all quests like that?

The Sketchbook
Of
Mia Quinn

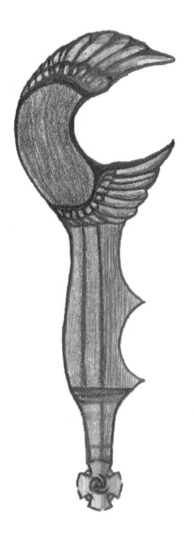

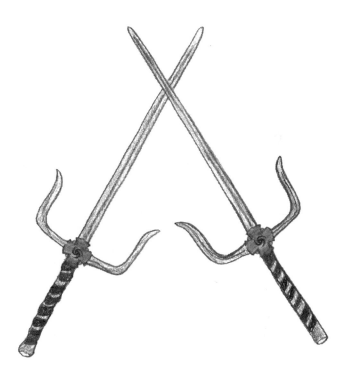

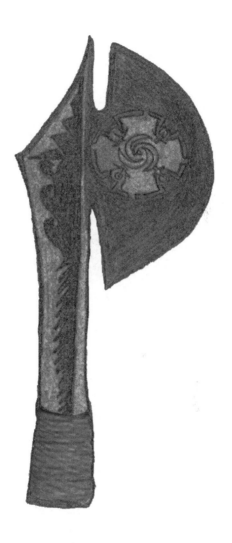

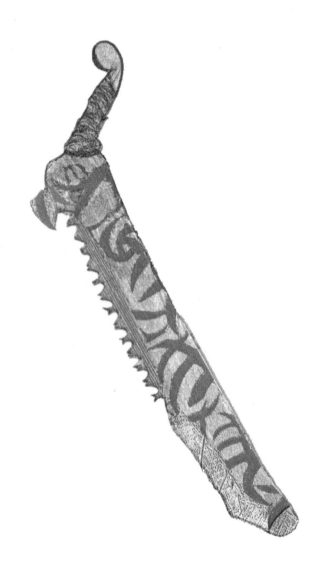

Elohim (el-o-heem)
Creator and Judge; He is the one and only true God; Elohim is the Hebrew word for God that occurs 2000 times in the Old Testament. It also refers to the plurality within the Godhead. (Genesis 1; Deuteronomy 4:39)

Yeshua (*yĕšūă*ʿ); **The Light**
Elohim came to earth in human form in the embodiment of His son, Jesus Christ. Yeshua is the Hebrew translation of Jesus-the light of the world. Yeshua chose twelve to follow him (disciples) and be His light unto the world. (John 3:16; John 8:12)

Dìonadain (di-o-na-dane)
Gaelic word meaning one who guards; legion of angels created by Elohim; act as watchers, guardians, messengers and warriors of the Light. (Psalms 91:11; Matthew 26:53)

Simon the Zealot
One of the twelve disciples (original Sorcha) chosen by Yeshua; tradition says he was martyred with a saw in Caistor, Lincolnshire, Britain around 61 A.D. (Matthew 10:2-4; Mark 10:2-4)

Sorcha (sor-sha)
Gaelic word meaning light (not dark); twelve human beings, possessing supernatural gifts, created by Elohim and chosen to embody the power of His Light in each generation (Genesis 1:26-28; Matthew 5:14-16; Matthew 10:2-4; 2 Peter 1:19-21)

Gifts of the Sorcha
The Dreamer (Daniel 1:17; Acts 2:17)
The Crafter (Exodus 31: 1-11; 2 Chronicles 2:12)
The Perceiver (1 Corinthians 12:10; 1 John 4: 1-6; 2)
The Believer (1 Corinthians 12:9; Hebrews 11:1)
The Healer (Acts 3:1-10; 1 Corinthians 12: 28)
The Wielder (Acts 5:12; Acts 19:11)
The Knower (Psalm 119:66; 1 Corinthians 12:8)
The Leader (2 Chronicles 1:7-12; Romans 12:6-8)
The Speaker (Mark 16:17-18; Acts 2:1-12)
The Warrior (Judges 13:24; 16:28; Philippians 4:13)
The Exiler (Mark 9:29; Luke 10:17)
The Psalter (2 Chronicles 20:21; Psalm 68:25)

The Natsar
Hebrew word for watchmen; meaning to guard, watch, preserve, keep, observe, to keep secret
(Isaiah 62:6; Jeremiah 4:16, 31:6)

Abaddon (ab-ah-don)
Hebrew word meaning destroyer; a fallen angel who rebelled against Elohim; the Prince of Darkness; roams the Earth seeking to destroy Elohim's creation, His Light, and the Sorcha. (Revelation 9:11, 12:9; Isaiah 14:12-15; 1 Peter 5:8-9)

Scàth (skahth)
Gaelic word meaning shadow; fallen angels who rebelled with Abaddon against Elohim; warriors of destruction; demons and malevolent spirits
(Ephesians 6:12; Jude 1:6; Revelation 12:9-11)

Mescàth (me-skahth)
Beings produced by the union of Scàth and Sorcha; at war with what lives within them, light and dark. (Genesis 6:4)

Gehenna (gi-**hen**-*uh)*
From the Greek *geenna* and from Hebrew *gehinnom;* hell, a place of fiery torment for the dead; the lake of fire; the valley of Hinnom, near Jerusalem, where children were sacrificed to Moloch. Jesus referred to Gehenna multiple times throughout New Testament scripture.
(II Kings 23:10; Jeremiah 7: 31, 19:2-6; Book of Matthew, Mark and Revelation)

Fiery Darts & Arrows
Weapon of the enemy
(Ephesians 6:16)

The Sorcha Books   **Volume 2: Unite**   **Reading Playlist**

Youthless by Beck
Dreamer by the Isbells
You Are the One Thing by Bright City
Piano Concerto No. 2 in C Minor, Op. 18: I. Moderato by Sergei Rachmaninov
Sound of Walking Away by Illenium
God's Gonna Cut You Down by Johnny Cash
Graceful Closure by Safe
Midnight by Coldplay
Brother by NEEDTOBREATHE
I Wouldn't Be by Kodaline
La Divina by Parov Stelar Trio
Tremble by Mosaic MSC
Snake Eyes by Mumford & Sons
Major Minus by Coldplay
Piano Sonata No. 14 in C-Sharp Minor, Op. 27 No. 2 "Moonlight Sonata" by Ludwig von Beethoven
The Watchtower by Sigimund

DIVE INTO THIS SNEAK PEEK OF

VANQUISH

VOLUME 3 OF THE SORCHA BOOKS

Lost in thought, the old man warmed his hands close to the fire. The light from the flames illuminated the map of wrinkles that spread across his aquiline face—a map that told of the old man's incredible journey. Each line was a sign of laughter, joy, smiles and affection. Each crevice was a road of sadness, worry, challenge and loss. His curious eyes watched the blazing fire.

From this hallowed and ancient place, he had watched. He had observed their perseverance and commitment, their folly and struggle. He had grieved when they were defeated. He had cheered when they had won a battle no matter how great or small. Each generation, however, had brought a time of sorrow and weeping. Too many seasons to number he had mourned— the loss of their lives, their gifts, and the long-awaited promise of the uniting of the Light.

He lifted his shoulders and sighed deeply. Once, he had imagined that time was his friend. Each day he had been given in his life afforded him the opportunity to do what needed to be done. Time was a gift from Elohim. With this gift, he, along with a small group of survivors from his village, had escaped Cain and built the fortress of Migdalah. Diligently, they had strategized for the protection of Simon's key and trained a company of watchmen, the Natsar. He had taken to heart the word of Elohim. He had numbered the days of his people since arriving on this icy isle so that they might gain hearts of wisdom. With great expectation, his people had watched for the awakening of the Sorcha, the power of their uniting and the arrival of the Light-bearers themselves.

As time blew across the frozen landscape of their remote island, he had decided his friend had become his foe. For centuries now, he had waited. Even still, he had refused to give up hope. There was a time for everything in Elohim's kingdom and a season for every activity under the heavens. There was a time to search and to give up, a time to keep and to throw away. He had held fast to this truth along with his purpose—guarding the key to his father's book. He would finish his task just like his father had before him. He would give his life if needed to fulfill his calling from Elohim. Tonight, however, the significance of time would cease to matter to him. He bowed his head to pray for the strength he knew he needed and would be given.

"Lord, the time for which you have prepared me has come. The task, given to me so long ago, is now no longer a burden to bear, but, a gift to give. Grant me wisdom. Order my steps. Strengthen my resolve. Allow me to measure and challenge the Light-bearers so that they may be ready for the battle before them. Elohim, thank you for the Light and its comfort to my people for all these many years. Amen."

He stood and made his way slowly through the winding passages of the Natsar's fortress. The tower was a bustle of activity—his people rife with the anticipation of a promise fulfilled. The cold northern air welcomed him with a blast as he walked through the heavy iron gate of the barbicon. Colorful lights shimmered and stretched across the silent sky. All at once, the light was a single path to heaven and the next it was an army of light marching north. When the great ram's horn sounded deep and strong from the turret above, he squared his shoulders and studied the horizon. Destiny. It echoed through the frigid vale. It settled in the frosty swirls of mist that blanketed the snow-capped mountains. It reflected in the jagged icy walls of the distant fjord. He felt the spirit of his father, Simon, next to him and it warmed his heart.

He closed his eyes thinking about the last night he had seen his father. Centuries had passed, yet now, standing in the glacial wind, he could still feel the erratic beat of his heart that night. When he had rapped on the door to his father's house, he had known already that time had run out. He laid his hand over his chest and remembered.

"Amhlaid, what is it?" his father asked quickly.

"We must go, Father. They are out for blood this time," he insisted, stepping across the threshold. "I have been watching the people in the neighboring village and someone has stirred their hatred against us. They are screaming sorcery and death for you."

Bowing his head, Simon said gravely. "I will not leave my people, my son."

"Please, Father, there's still time for us to flee," he begged earnestly. "You and mother must come with me. The gates will never hold against the crowd marching upon us now."

Walking back into the room, Simon untied the binding and unrolled the scroll he had just completed on the rough-hewn table. The pages glowed warmly in the lamplight.

He gasped. "You have finished, father."

Simon pulled one of the pages from the rest and then bound the scroll again. He tied the single page he had removed with a worn piece of leather and offered it to him.

"*Keep it safe, no matter the cost, even if it means your own life,*" *his father said with conviction.* "*It is the key to understanding what I have written. The twelve will find you when it is time. Go now, quickly, my dearest son.*"

He took the scroll without question. His father had prepared him as best he could for what was surely to come. Simon kissed his forehead in blessing and he fled into the thick mist of the dawn.

Ahmlaid opened his eyes. "I kept it safe, father," he whispered. "Our time has come. The Sorcha are finally here."

About The Authors

• • •

Susan Alford, author and educator, is a psychology professor at Lee University in Cleveland, Tennessee where she lives with her husband and two daughters.

Lesley Smith, author, singer and pastor's wife, resides in Atlanta, Georgia with her husband and their two daughters.

Candace Alford, illustrator, is a freelance artist, graphic designer and a passionate advocate for her son and raising awareness for those who have autism.

The imaginations and spiritual lives of the sisters were ignited as children, when they listened to their grandparents' tales about angels and demons. This background gave rise to the Sorcha books. Sorcha: Unite is the sequel to Sorcha: Awaken, which was an Amazon Top 100 best seller and appeared on Amazon's top ten list of Christian fantasy books.

Made in the USA
Lexington, KY
28 April 2018